"A per ___ th this
amazin, ___

"This ___ ___ k Blog
passion ___ ___ it and

___ Sheets
"I have ___ k you,
Nelle, ___ ty, and
most of ___ eviews

"It is o ___ eviews

"Nelle ___ . . in a
way tha ___ thered.
The act ___ ite the
page-tu ___ eaders
look fo ___

___ eviews

"The c ___ ed the
epilogu ___ ke and
his tige ___

___ viewer

"I can' ___ ltimate
book b

—*Book Boyfriend Reviews*

"I just loved this installment. You can feel the emotions pour out from each side. This was such a great series, and I wish there was more."

—*Wicked Reads Review Team*

BOOKS BY NELLE L'AMOUR

Seduced by the Park Avenue Billionaire

Strangers on a Train (Part 1)
Derailed (Part 2)
Final Destination (Part 3)
Seduced by the Park Avenue Billionaire (Box Set)

An Erotic Love Story

Undying Love (Book 1)

Gloria

Gloria's Secret (Book 1)
Gloria's Revenge (Book 2)
Gloria's Forever (Book 2.5)

That Man Trilogy

THAT MAN 1
THAT MAN 2
THAT MAN 3

THAT MAN 3

THAT

MAN

3

NELLE L'AMOUR

That Man 3
Copyright © 2014 by Nelle L'Amour
Print Edition
All rights reserved worldwide
First Edition: May 2014

Nelle L'Amour thanks you for your understanding and support. To join her mailing list for new releases, please sign up here: http://eepurl.com/N3AXb

NICHOLS CANYON PRESS
Los Angeles, CA USA

THAT MAN 3
By Nelle L'Amour

ISBN-13: 978-1500408817
ISBN-10: 1500408816

Cover by Arijana Karcic, Cover It! Designs
Proofreading by Karen Lawson
Formatting by BB eBooks

To everyone who has dared to do something out of their comfort zone. This book is for you.

And to my daughters, who I hope will make daring choices in their lives that will bring them closer to the truth of who they are.

THAT MAN 3

Chapter 1

Blake

The shuttle from Friedman Memorial Airport in Hadley to the Sun Valley Lodge, where I was staying over the Christmas break, took fifteen minutes. Leaving my rollaway bag and skis with the valet, I headed inside to the check-in counter and took in my surroundings. The lobby of the venerable resort, built in 1936, was decked out for Christmas with a huge, almost ceiling high lit up tree and a roaring fire in the massive, holly-trimmed hearth. The place was bustling with guests milling around the lobby, hot drinks in their hands. Christmas music was playing over the speaker system. It was a winter wonderland.

Fortunately, the check-in line was short, and I was able to handle my reservation quickly. As the jolly attendant handed me my key card, a warm breath tickled my neck and a familiar, seductive voice traveled through my ear.

"Hi, Blakey."

I spun around. Fuck. It was Kirstie. Or was it Kristie? I could never tell those two apart. She was dressed in skinny faded jeans, a tight turtleneck sweater that clung to her D-cup boobs, and pink Uggs. Her platinum hair cascaded over her shoulders from beneath a matching pink ski hat.

"I didn't know you'd be here." My voice wavered. Why wasn't I excited to see her? She was as drop-dead gorgeous as ever and ready to be laid.

She moved uncomfortably close, trapping me between the counter and her body. Her heavy floral scent was suffocating me. She smelled nothing of cherries and vanilla.

She licked her billowy glossed lips. They looked bigger than the last time I saw them. "Yeah. My sister and I got in last night. Why don't we get in some ski time together?"

"Sure. Let me get settled into my room, and we'll head to the slopes." I immediately regretted what I said. I wanted to ski alone.

"What room are you in?"

I glanced down at my key card. "Room 606."

"Cool. Kirstie and I are right next door." Well, at least, I now knew which one she was. However, the thought of having the Barbie doll twins a wall apart was unsettling. Too close for comfort.

"Want me to help you check in?" she breathed, circling her big tits against my ski jacket. Her implants made her nipples so hard and erect I could feel them through the thick down-lined fabric. I squirmed as far away from her as I could.

"I can handle it. I'll meet you down here in a half hour, and we'll head over to Baldy." Baldy was my favorite place to ski with its elevation of over nine thousand feet and myriad of blazing trails.

"Perfect," she purred.

She sashayed away and I heaved a sigh of relief.

My suite consisted of a bedroom with an adjacent bathroom, a living room with a fireplace, and a kitchenette. It was decorated in what I'd call Alpine-themed Ralph Lauren. Mirroring the lobby, the décor was floral, with the king-sized bed, couch, and curtains all done up in a red and pine green leafy print. Wall-to-wall dark green carpet lined the floor.

I listlessly unpacked my suitcase, putting the jeans and heavy sweaters I'd brought along into a set of drawers. The rest of my skiwear I hung up in the closet. I should have been excited about being in Sun Valley—I'd always had a great time here with all the fabulous activities the charming town offered, not the least being getting laid morning, noon and night, but instead I felt blue. I fucking missed Jennifer and wished she were here with me. All during my flight, I kept thinking about her. Hoping she was thinking about me. I hadn't seen or spoken to her since our gift exchange at the office yesterday. Carefully, I set the last item in my suitcase on top of my nightstand. The little snow globe she'd given me. I gave it a shake and watched the glittery snowflakes flutter over the golden ball that somehow reminded me of my grandma's matzo balls. The memory of watching her eat one at my parents' Shabbat dinner flashed into my head. I'd fantasized her sensuous mouth on one of my balls and had almost come in my pants. She'd given the expression "from soup to nuts" a whole new meaning. And then my mind jumped forward to the other night. The night of the office Christmas party—the night we fucked our brains out. It was the best sex I'd ever had. And I'd had a lot. But it was more than the sex. While I could have fucked her one more time, I could have held her in my arms forever. I thought the feeling was mutual. But it wasn't. To my utter shock, she didn't want me. She said she'd made a mistake. That I'd taken advantage of her in her vulnerable state. A rebound fuck after her jolting breakup with her fiancé, that two-timing dentist. Dickwick. Plus, she was afraid of having an office relationship. At least, that I could understand. If it didn't work out and one of us was going to get fired— who was it going to be? Her or me, the big *jefe's* son? You guessed right. With his dreams of having me head up his media empire, my father would never fire me from Conquest Broadcasting.

But then I really fucked up. Big time. Desperate, I

told her we could be casual fuck buddies. I honestly didn't mean it, but she didn't believe me. She got dressed and left me. Alone in my fuck pad with no one to fuck.

Never having dealt with rejection, I was fucking devastated. And confused. Selfish, spoiled, alpha me was a player. I left girls and not vice versa. They wanted me and couldn't get enough of me. But not Jennifer McCoy. I had succeeded magnificently and failed miserably.

Her reaction to the gift I'd given her—the erotic painting of a kiss by Jaime Zander's late father that mirrored our own first, unforgettable kiss—had given me a little hope. She was overwhelmed. And not because it was such an extravagant gift. My father always said actions speak louder than words. And he was right. The painting brought tears to her glimmering green eyes because it hit a nerve deep inside her. It made her feel something. The same thing I felt. The electricity in the air between us was so thick you could see sparks flying. It had taken all I had not to haul her into my arms, smother her with another all-consuming kiss, and fuck her senseless over my desk. And then just hold her in my arms.

She was right—we needed time away from each other to figure things out. Or at least she did. With a weighty heart, I gave the snow globe another shake and made a wish. I wished my tiger would come to the same conclusion as me: we plain and simply belonged together. With a twitch, my hopeful cock toasted to that. But deep inside my soul, I knew a relationship was a remote possibility. I sucked at them. In fact, I'd never had one.

Donning my ski gear, I clunked downstairs to the lobby in my heavy ski boots, my skis and poles under my arms. Kristie was already in the lobby. She was all dolled up in an expensive hot pink fur-trimmed ski jacket and matching ski pants. Furry earmuffs covered her ears, and she wore a thick layer of pink lipstick in the exact shade of her outfit. I didn't want that lipstick anywhere near me, but she was all over me before I could say, "fuck off." I finally managed to pull my lips away from hers without creating a scene. I thought about stopping at the concierge and asking for an antiseptic wipe on my way out. The thought of having to share a chairlift with her was repulsive.

We took the shuttle and got to Baldy in no time. There was a long line for the lift. While we waited for a chair, my bubbly companion babbled on non-stop about all the fun she and her twin sister had had so far from ice skating to skinny dipping in the heated pool. She boasted how everyone recognized them from their print ads and commercials. For sure, a movie offer would be coming soon. I half-listened, interjecting an occasional "wow" or "cool." My mind was elsewhere. Focused on someone else. My tiger. She was roaring in my head.

I was actually glad there was a wait for the lift because I dreaded getting on it with bubblehead. She had no control over her sexual appetite nor did her sister. Up until now, I couldn't get enough of the titillating twins alone or together—they were perfect hook-up material—but something inside me had changed. Let's cut to the chase. Some sweet little Midwestern girl with a dimpled smile had shown me there was something more. There was a connection between my cock and my heart. And she was in my bloodstream bringing them together. Making me feel emotions and sensations I'd never felt with anyone.

After twenty long, cold minutes, we finally got a chairlift meant for two. The temperature had dropped significantly, and the sky had turned an angry shade of gray. It looked like it was going to snow. I followed Kristie into the lift and sat as far away from her as I could. That didn't last long. After I lowered the safety bar and hung up our skis, she scooched across the seat until she was almost sitting on my lap. I jumped when her hand reached for my fly and pulled it down. Peeling off her gloves, she reached under my briefs and grabbed my dick.

"Fuck off, Kristie!" I forcefully yanked her hand off and zipped up my fly.

She looked miffed. "What bug do you have up your ass?"

"I'm just not in the mood." My voice was as bitter cold as the air.

"Fine." She stabbed the word at me and scooted away.

Relieved, I took in the spectacular view of the snow-covered mountains and trees through my goggles as our chair made its ascent. And wished I could share it with Jen.

When we reached the top of the trail, Kristie jumped off the lift. "Fuck you, Blake. Ski by yourself." She zoomed off.

For the first time since I'd gotten here, I smiled.

Usually I zipped down the advanced Black Diamond trail, expertly maneuvering its sharp twists and turns, but today I took my time zigzagging on my skis through the powder-perfect snow. The skier's high I usually got was not possible with Jennifer on my mind. I longed to be with her on the bunny slope. Teaching her how to ski . . . holding her as she awkwardly snow ploughed down the little hill . . . hearing her little gasps and then scream when she lost control . . . and helping her back on her feet when she tumbled onto the white powder. My heart ached to have her in my arms, feel her warm lips on mine, and indulge in all the après-ski activities made for lovers—from sitting in a hot Jacuzzi under the stars to sharing a blanket on a horse and carriage ride through town.

The biting wind whipped across my face as I made my way downward. About a quarter way down the slope, it began to snow, and by the time I was halfway down, the flurries had morphed into a blinding blizzard. Distracted, it took all I had to focus and circumvent the obscured trees and other obstacles along the way. I was relieved to reach the bottom. While many avid skiers were going back up despite the storm, I'd had enough. Removing my skis, I caught the next shuttle to the hotel.

It was three o'clock when I got back to the lodge. Leaving my skis in storage, I headed to my suite, where I disrobed and took a hot bath after calling room service. Not having much of an appetite, I ordered a hot toddy to soothe away the mental pain that was coursing through my veins.

Soaking in the large steamy tub, I stretched my legs out and studied my dick. It was limp. I swear Mr. Burns was wearing a sad face. He'd never been in this state before. Desperate, yes; despondent, no. Wanking off was not going to solve the problem.

"Don't worry. I'm going to figure out how to get you back with Jennifer." Fuck. What was wrong with me? I was talking to my dick. It stirred as if it had heard me. Stepping out of the tub, I towel dried my pal gently. The poor guy. He hung low and lifeless.

"Call her," I heard Mr. Burns whimper in my head.

"I can't," I said aloud. I'd promised her I wouldn't. Unless it was a business-related emergency. Nonetheless, I had the burning urge to break my promise. To hear her sweet voice. To tell her I missed her. Terribly. I'd never missed a woman before. This was a whole new feeling for me. It was as if I'd had been kicked in the balls.

No, I couldn't call her. It would be a mistake. We needed time apart to figure things out. Except I'd already done that. I wanted her to be mine.

With an empty heart, I shrugged on the fluffy terry cloth robe that came with the room. By the time I knotted the belt, I had a change of mind. Fuck it. I was going to call her. I needed to hear her voice. I needed to tell her something important.

I dashed back into the bedroom to get my cell phone. I thought I'd left it on my night table, but it wasn't there. Balls. Where the hell had I put it? I frantically searched everywhere—tearing the room apart. I also checked the pockets of everything I'd worn. *Nada.* Fuck. Fuck. Fuck. Where was it? Finally, I spotted it—under the bed. It must have fallen out of my ski pants when I took them off. As I bent down to retrieve it, a loud knock sounded at the door. *Room service.* I ran to the door and opened it.

"Room service."

I gaped.

"My sister told me you were here."

Christ. It was the other twin—Kirstie, dressed in a long fur coat that must have cost a fortune and mile-high black leather stiletto boots.

"I hope you like your pussy moist and raw." With a flutter of her false eyelashes, she flung open her coat, exposing her bare body—tit, stock, and barrel. In a breath, she was all over me, gnawing and grappling every ounce of flesh she could find.

I found my voice and shoved her away. "Kirstie, get the fuck out of here."

"What's wrong with you?" she growled. She was as clueless as her bimbo sister but more aggressive, not letting my words get in the way. She fisted my hair and bit down on my lips. I pushed her away again, knocking her flat against the wall.

While she stood there fuming, I knew what I had to do. I hurried to the room phone and dialed the concierge.

"I'm the one who should be calling security," hissed the presumptuous twin.

Not responding to her, I told the concierge to book me the next flight to Boise.

"We're sorry, Mr. Burns. The airport is closed due to the storm. There won't be any flights available until tomorrow."

Fuck. I couldn't wait that long. "Then get me a rental car right away."

Good news. There was one available. I slammed the receiver back on the cradle and then frantically gathered up all my belongings, including my cell phone. I threw everything into my suitcase. Before closing it, I yanked out my jeans, a tee, and a heavy Nordic sweater plus a pair of after-ski boots. And a hat.

Five minutes later, I was dressed and almost out the door. "You can have the room; it'll be good for you not to share something with your sister," I told the dumbstruck blonde. She stood wide-mouthed against the wall, watching me as I split.

Fifteen minutes later, I was heading south on Highway 75, driving through a bitch of a blizzard in the four-wheel drive Jeep I'd rented. With the inclement weather conditions, the concierge had told me the 150-mile trip would take close to four hours. Maybe more because I made one stop in Ketchum to pick up a few things. Thank you, Jesus. The stores were open late on Christmas Eve to accommodate last minute shoppers. God bless American consumerism.

I'd done a lot of crazy things in my life, but this was by far the craziest. Despite being tethered with chains, the SUV inched along the icy road, sliding and spinning out of control. My hands gripped the steering wheel like iron clamps while every muscle in my body clenched. To make things worse, the windshield wipers couldn't keep up with the rapidly falling mega flakes of snow. It was impossible to see ahead or behind me. It was all one big white blur. Only one thing was clear: I was risking my life. But Jennifer McCoy, my little tiger, was worth it.

Chapter 2

Jennifer

It felt good to be home. Our neighborhood in the North End section of Boise hadn't changed a bit. The people who lived there and the homes they lived in were straight out of a Norman Rockwell painting. Middle America at its finest. So different from hectic, multi-ethnic Los Angeles.

Dad had picked me up at noon at the airport in his station wagon and couldn't be happier to see me. The feeling was mutual. I was a daddy's girl and loved my father. Of course, he was surprised Bradley wasn't with me. I told him there'd been a change in plans and that I would explain everything to him and Mom when we got to the house. Fortunately, he didn't press further.

"Mom's made your favorite gingerbread cookies," he said as we passed by rows of shingled cookie-cutter homes all decked out with Christmas lights and decorations. "We're all going to make a gingerbread house later." Making one of these elaborate holiday confections was a family tradition.

I studied my father as he drove. Having recently

retired from university life at the age of sixty-five, he looked as handsome as ever to me. Though wrinkles lined his face and his hair was now flecked with gray, his sage-green eyes twinkled behind his scholarly horn-rimmed glasses, and a warm smile radiated on his face.

In no time, we pulled up to our stately red brick house. It was one of the best decorated houses on the street. Strings of bright blinking lights outlined the framework and windows, and a charming manger scene sat on the front lawn. There was also a large wreath on the red-painted front door. Dad parked the car in the garage and helped me with my suitcase. Holding the large shopping bag that contained my parents' Christmas presents, I followed my father eagerly through the door to our house. The smell of freshly baked bread wafted up my nose. I was home.

"Darling!" exclaimed my mother as I set foot in the kitchen. Wearing a floral-patterned apron, she ran over to hug me before I had a chance to shrug off my coat or put down the bag. She looked prettier than ever. Her gray-blue eyes sparkled, and her short ash-brown hair was now chin-length and held back by a red velvet band.

"Where's Bradley?"

The million-dollar question. I took a deep breath and the words tumbled out. "We broke up."

The look on her face went from joyful to alarmed. "Goodness gracious! Are you all right, darling? You look like you've lost weight." The tone of her voice bordered on panic.

"I'm fine." Without going into details, I told her that I'd discovered Bradley was cheating on me with his hygienist. Why beat around the bush?

My mother gasped. "Good Lord! How did you find out?"

"Caught him in the act." I didn't want to tell them about the video footage; it was simpler with this mild white lie. Well, it was almost the truth. "I gave him back his ring."

"You poor thing," exclaimed my mother, stroking my hair. I was grateful she didn't probe for details.

My father remained pensively silent and then uttered one word: "Shmuck."

My father said shmuck?

"Jennie baby, you can do better."

Good is the enemy of better. Blake's father's favorite expression whirled around in my head. And in a millisecond, the image of my sexy, beautiful boss was spinning there too. I hadn't stopped missing him. Last night, I'd barely slept a wink. Tears pricked my eyes each time I relived opening his gift. He'd given me a precious piece of artwork. A painting that had moved me to tears. *The Kiss.* I couldn't stop thinking about it. I knew why Blake had bought it for me. It symbolized us. Two lovers entwined in a passionate embrace. I still wasn't over the shocking discovery that Blake—my boss—was *that* man I'd kissed blindfolded in a game of Truth or Dare on the night of my engagement party. He'd kissed me again at the office Christmas party, and from there, we'd surrendered our bodies to each other. He'd made me feel things I'd never felt. *Ecstasy!* Yet, I had to break away, knowing that Blake was bad for me in every way. The painting, however, had changed everything. It had turned my heart upside down and torn me apart. I could no longer deny my feelings. I missed him for only one reason. I was in love.

My mother's gentle voice intercepted my thoughts as well as a fresh batch of tears. "Darling, why don't you settle into your room and then come down for some lunch? I've made your favorite vegetable soup and baked a loaf of bread."

"Sure, Mom," I said, my voice unsteady. My father insisted on bringing up my bag, but I told him I could handle it myself. I needed alone time.

Glumly, I trudged upstairs to my room. I unpacked the bag and then stood by my bedroom window. I peered outside. The sky was already darkening and, in fact, looked ominous. Perhaps, it was going to snow. In the distance, I could see the snow-capped mountains, and another pang of sadness stabbed at my heart. Blake was somewhere in those mountains. I shuddered at the thought of him surrounded by a dozen blond ski bunnies. I'm sure Mr. Player was in his element and already getting laid. A wicked thought crossed my mind. Maybe an avalanche would bury his bimbos.

My wishful thinking was short-lived. A tear escaped my eyes. I suddenly regretted not accepting his offer to spend the day with him and telling him not to contact me—unless it was a business emergency. Without warning, the floodgates broke loose, and tears cascaded down my face. Who was I kidding? I desperately wanted to hear his voice. Inhale his intoxicating scent And most of all, be held in his arms and kissed by those lips.

Trying to get my mind off Blake, I spent the rest of the day reading an e-book, running errands with my mom, and baking Christmas goodies. We assembled the gingerbread house and put the final touches on our Christmas tree, which stood tall and noble by our living room window, replete with charming ornaments my mother had collected over her lifetime. The fresh pine scent of the tree mixed with that of the delicacies my mother was forever baking and made the house smell delicious.

Yet, no matter how much I busied myself, nothing could distract me from thinking about Blake. In the short time I'd been home, my feelings for him had intensified instead of diminished. *Absence makes the heart grow fonder*, my mother had always told me whenever Dad was away on an academic conference. She would keep her eyes glued on the kitchen wall clock until he returned. Count down the days, the hours, the minutes. Even the seconds.

I missed Blake. Plain and simple. Much like my mom did with my dad. I thought about him every minute, every second of the afternoon . . . what he was doing . . . what he was wearing (or not) . . . who he was with. The image of him surrounded by his O.K. Corral—his bevy of blond beauties—made my stomach clench and sent my heartbeat into a frenzy. *Absence makes the heart wander.* The other side of the equation. I wrestled with the idea of calling him, but that would be breaking my own rule. Rules sucked.

Late in the afternoon, while I was baking sugar cookies with my mom, she noticed my anxiousness. It bordered on despondency.

"Honey, you seem a little on edge," she commented, mixing a bowl of batter.

"I'm fine." My voice faltered. I made up an excuse—something about Bradley. Truthfully, he was the last person on my mind. I did, however, secretly wish for Santa to bring him coal; that's what Dickwick deserved. Upon taking a tray of cookies out of the oven, I burnt my middle finger. Served me right for my wicked thought.

Christmas Eve came quickly. My mother was preparing her traditional meal with my help. Taking a break once everything was in the oven, I played a game of Scrabble with my dad. It was hard to beat the former English professor. Plus, I had a rack full of shitty low-point letters. Then I spotted an opportunity. The word I had in mind sent a rush of flutters to my core.

"O-R-G-A-S-M-I-C," I spelled out, using all my tiles. In addition to scoring fifteen points for the word, I earned another fifty bonus points for using all my tiles. A grand total of sixty-five points. I smiled smugly at my dad. I was now significantly ahead of him. I might even win the game. I had Blake to thank.

My father's brows shot up. I think it was more in response to the word than my feat. "Good one," he muttered. My victory, however, was short-lived when he laid out all his tiles and spelled the word "EXQUIS-ITE." In addition to also accruing fifty bonus points, he got double and triple letter scores for the eight-point "X" and ten-point "Q" plus a double word score for a total of two hundred twenty points.

"Sheesh, Dad," I moaned. *Two hundred and twenty points.* It had to be a new *Guinness Book of Records* high. No matter what I did, I could never beat my dad at Scrabble.

The sound of Christmas music outside our house stopped me from contemplating my next word. Of course, it was carolers—a group of locals from our church who made it a yearly tradition to go house to house on Christmas Eve.

My mother heard them too and dashed out of the kitchen. Together, we hurried to our front door. My father opened it, and the carolers, which included several children, stood before our house. It was hard to distinguish their faces because there was a thick layer of fog. And snowflakes were falling. I caught one with my tongue. Wouldn't that be something—a white Christmas?

My parents and I huddled together in the doorway as the carolers sang a succession of traditional Christmas songs. I loved Christmas music; it moved me to tears. Every which way it was sung—be it traditional renditions of the songs or contemporary rock ones, instrumental or acapella. My favorite of all was *The Little Drummer Boy*, which, to my delight, they sang before dispersing to the next house.

After the carolers departed, my parents retreated to the living room while I remained motionless at the doorway. There was one remaining lone caroler.

He stood tall before me, his hands tucked in the pockets of his heavy down jacket. A knit ski cap with reindeer antlers covered his head, and somehow that silly hat made him look more heart-stoppingly adorable than ever. My heart drummed against my chest and then jumped into my throat. My eyes clicked open and shut like a camera lens, taking a snapshot of this moment I wanted to keep forever. It was him. *That* man who made me delirious with lust and desire. Blake!

A giant lump swelled in my throat as he sang, "All I Want for Christmas is You." His sexy, raspy voice resonated like a rock star. *My* rock star! Tears poured from my eyes as I broke into a broad smile. In the background, I could hear my mother yelling, "Jennifer, close the door. It's freezing in here."

I was on fire. I could no longer contain myself. Before he could finish the song, I bolted out of the house and ran up to him—in my sweats and barefoot. He swept me into his arms and swung me around and around. As the flakes of snow danced in the moonlight, his lips latched onto mine in a fierce, passionate kiss I wanted never to end.

"What are you doing here?" I managed, my arms clinging to him, my mouth hungrily gnawing at every visible ounce of flesh I could find.

He held me tight. A puff of his breath warmed the icy air. "Oh, tiger. Don't you know?"

"Know what?" I gasped, gripping his scarf.

"I'm crazy about you."

My eyes searched his face. "Meaning what?" He *was* a little insane.

"Meaning I can't bear to be away from you."

"Meaning . . . ?"

My heart literally stopped as I awaited his response.

"Meaning I'm fucking in love with you, Jennifer McCoy."

Hot tears fell from my eyes as the frigid night air shot through me. Trembling, I struggled to get words out. "How do you know that?"

He tilted up my chin with his soft leather-gloved hand. My watering eyes met his; not a blink. He licked a snowflake off my cheek before my tears melted it.

"Because your needs come before mine."

My words! What I had once told him when he'd asked what it meant to be in love. Sobs mixed with laughter. I shivered.

"Baby, you're cold." He drew me closer to him, blanketing me in the warmth of his strong arms and snuggly down jacket. I pressed my head against his chest as he held me tightly. He gently kissed the top of my head and then I looked up and held his beautiful face in my gaze. Passion danced in his eyes.

"Mr. Burns, I only have one need." *One word.* "You."

His face broke out in that dazzling dimpled smile. Yanking off his wooly hat, he lowered it over my head and then wrapped his scarf around my neck. "And that's why I'm here. You're my world, baby. You're everything to me. *Everything.*" His lips crashed back onto mine, and despite the freezing temperature, I melted into him.

"Jennie McCoy! What are you doing outside in your bare feet? You're going to catch pneumonia!"

At the sound of my father's voice, I hastily pulled away from Blake. "I love you too," I whispered before responding to my father who was standing in the doorway. I was sure he hadn't witnessed our embrace.

"Dad, this is a friend from work, who by coincidence, happens to be in town."

"Hi," said Blake cheerfully with a wave of his hand. I had to stifle my giggles.

"Well, don't just stand out there and freeze. Invite him in." My father headed back inside the house.

I could no longer contain my laughter when Blake scooped me up into his arms and carried me to the front door. His lips smothered mine. In my whole life, I'd never been happier.

Blake's mother had her famous brisket; my mother had her famous Irish stew. It was what she made every year for Christmas Eve dinner, and I never got tired of it. A hearty blend of beef, potatoes, carrots, and onions that she marinated overnight in a secret-ingredient beer-based broth, it was melt-in-your-mouth scrumptious. She promised when I got married she would share the recipe; I was just going to have to wait longer than I thought.

Just before we sat down for dinner, Blake ran to his rental car that he'd parked down the street. When he returned, he was covered with a fine layer of snow and carrying three oversized shopping bags. He withdrew three beautifully wrapped boxes from the two largest and placed them under our tree. The third one he handed to my father.

"I thought you might enjoy these at dinner," Blake said as my father removed the contents.

Fine wine. California Cabernet—not one, but two bottles.

"How thoughtful of you, Blake dear," chimed my mother.

"My pleasure." Blake beamed like a proud Boy Scout who'd had just received his first medal of honor.

Smiling, my father examined the labels on the bottles. "A Napa Valley Select Reserve from 1990. An excellent year. The year our darling daughter was born."

I felt my cheeks turn as red as the wine. Blake did everything right. Everything to rouse me. He shot me a saucy smile and made me heat up more.

Dinner was served in our dining room. The table was festive. My mother used her special holiday china. Votive candles and colorful Christmas balls were scattered across the poinsettia-print tablecloth. The velvety wine flowed freely, and everyone ate as if there were no tomorrow. I could tell my mother was pleased Blake adored her stew; he even asked for seconds. He was a far cry from Bradley for whom my mother had once painstakingly cooked a special vegan meal—most of which he didn't eat.

Blake also bonded with my father over college football and was familiar with the Boise State Broncos. To my relief, he avoided talking about work—and no mention was made of heading a porn channel where I worked. Phew! My parents had no clue. I sure didn't need to give them both coronaries on Christmas Eve.

I was in heaven. My eyes made subtle contact with Blake's every chance I had. My body was aflutter; every nerve was buzzing. I couldn't believe he was here celebrating Christmas Eve with me. And I couldn't believe he was in love with me. And I with him. Blake Burns, my boss. *That* man who'd I kissed blindfolded in a game of Truth or Dare. *That* man who'd consumed my lips once again under a bough of mistletoe. And then fucked my brains out and had given me what I thought was the best present of my life. A painting I'd coveted called *The Kiss*. There was only one present better. More powerful. More precious. The gift of his love.

Someone pinch me. Under the table, two fingers did. Blake's. The way they'd pinched me at the Conquest Christmas party—right on my clit. I jumped in my seat a little, hoping in one breath he would behave himself in front of my parents, and in another, hoping he'd finger me until I could no longer sit still. For better or for worse, Mr. Burns behaved. Well sort of.

"How did you find our house?" I asked.

He grinned and fed me his familiar line. "Where there's a will, there's a way."

"Come on, tell us," I pleaded as he continued to scissor my clit. Beneath my dress, I was a hot wet mess. I forced myself to take another bite of my mother's stew. My parents were all ears.

"I came across some carolers. They told me they'd be passing by. So I followed them."

"Very clever, Mr. Burns." My clit on fire, I squirmed in my chair. *Oh was he!*

My mother smiled. "So nice of you to come."

At the word "come," a massive orgasm assaulted me. I choked on the mouthful of stew I was swallowing. I quickly washed it down with some wine.

"Are you okay, darling?" asked my concerned mother. My father's brows furrowed.

"Yes," I gulped. At least, the near-choking reflex had covered up my reaction to what'd just happened. Catching my breath, I knew my face was as red as a poinsettia. Blake shot me an innocent glance. I loved and hated him. Scratch that. I so loved him. The glow in his eyes sent me the same message.

Dinner culminated with my mother's delicious bread pudding, served along with coffee and brandy.

Blake devoured the dessert and once again asked for a second helping to my mother's delight.

"I should be heading back to my hotel," he said, scooping up the last morsel of the yummy pudding.

My heart sunk.

"Where you are staying?" asked my dad.

"At The Grove."

The Grove, located downtown, coincidentally shared the name of the Los Angeles mall where I'd purchased all my Christmas presents. It was one of the most luxurious hotels in Boise but truthfully paled in comparison to Blake's parents' mansion.

He pushed back his chair and stood up. My mother excused herself to bring him his ski jacket. My father rose to shake his hand. "A pleasure to have you here, Blake." The genuine smile they shared put one of my own on my face. Dad liked Blake.

We accompanied Blake to the front door. The romantic tension between us was thick. My clit still throbbing, I didn't want him to leave. To our surprise, when we opened the door, it was now blizzarding. The wind whipped through the frigid air as a whirling dervish of white flakes fell from the sky. The streets were already blanketed with a foot of snow. If not more.

My mother reacted first. "Blake, dear, you can't drive into town with all this snow. The streets are icy. And you won't be able to see three feet ahead of you."

My dad chimed in, "Son." *Son?* "My wife is right. It's way too dangerous to drive. We're not even going to midnight Mass. Stay here with us tonight."

Mom: "Absolutely. We have a lovely spare bedroom right next to Jennifer's. A guest room."

"Are you sure?" asked Blake, blinking in the fortuitous white flakes. "I don't want to be an imposition."

"Absolutely," my parents responded in unison.

"Thank you." He grinned that heart-stopping smile and then slipped me a wink.

Reality hit me with the force of Santa's sleigh. Blake was staying overnight, and tomorrow, Christmas morning, I would wake up to him here in my house.

Reality wasn't as bad as everyone thought. It didn't get better than having a white Christmas with the man you loved.

Chapter 3

Blake

The guest room with its matching floral bedspread and curtains couldn't have been cozier. But there was no way I could fall asleep with the girl I loved tucked in a bed in the room right next to mine. My cock was craving a different kind of cozy.

"Hello, Mr. Burns," I said as it sprung free from my pajama bottoms. I wrapped my hands around my girth and gripped it as if I were shaking someone's hand. "I'm going to make you hard and then we're going on a little adventure." Filling my mind with the glorious image of Jennifer naked, I ran my hand up and down my shaft until it grew thick and rigid. It took no time. I reached for the condom on my night table, ripped open the foil with my teeth, and slipped it over my tower of steel. I fixed my pajamas and grabbed the little box sitting on the nightstand next to my snow globe. Jennifer was about to get her first Christmas present from Santa. Ho, Ho, Ho.

Bare-chested, I stealthily slipped out of my room, making sure that neither Mr. nor Mrs. McCoy was roaming the hallway. The coast was clear. I tiptoed over to Jennifer's room, and while I thought about knocking first, I simply turned the doorknob. The door creaked opened. I chortled silently. My tiger had left it unlocked. For sure, intentionally even if she didn't know it.

"Hi."

Startled, Jennifer, who was propped up against her fluffy pillows reading something on her Kindle, jolted.

Standing at the doorway, I took in her room. It was totally princessy—pink, pink and more pussy pink—with a canopy bed and shag carpet. Along with her college degrees, a large framed poster of SpongeBob, her favorite cartoon character, hung on a wall. Scattered on her dresser were some framed photos of her and her parents. Pigtailed, she was an adorable little girl, and she was even more adorable now, I thought as I inhaled the sweet scent of cherries and vanilla.

"Blake! What are you doing here?" she gasped as I made my way to her bed after kicking the door shut and locking it.

"What does it look like? I'm getting into bed with you," I responded, squeezing into her tiny twin bed before she had a chance to notice my hard-on. I snuggled next to her. Man, this bed was barely big enough for one person, let alone two.

"You can't sleep here! What if my parents come in?"

"They won't, and besides, I've locked the door."

"What if I still say no? Are you going to fuck me into submission?"

My cock flexed and a cocky smile curled on my lips. "That's Plan B."

Her eyes widened. "What's Plan A?"

One of my hands came up from under the cover. In it was the small gift box wrapped in hot pink paper and topped off with a small silver bow. I had kept it hidden behind my back when I'd crept into her room.

"What's that?"

"It's just a small Christmas present."

A combination of guilt and curiosity flickered in her green-as-a-Christmas-tree eyes. "You're making me feel bad. I don't have anything else to give you. I mean, I didn't know—"

I cut her off. "Don't worry, you'll be giving me what I wished for on Christmas shortly. Now, open it up."

"It's from Gloria's Secret," she commented, noticing the famous heart logo on the paper. "Sexy lingerie?"

While that would have been a fine gift too, one I would have bit off her sweet ass, this one was way more creative. And it was going to be way more fun.

"No. Just open it." She was making my cock twitch with anticipation. I watched as she carefully tore off the wrapping. She stared blankly at the package. "What is this, Blake?"

"It's a toy. You can't have Christmas without getting a toy."

"My Secret Egg?"

"It's a sex toy. You're going to love playing with it. Open the package."

She fumbled getting the box open. I think I already had her aroused.

She lifted the sparkly little pink egg out of the carton and examined it.

"I was almost going to get you a regular vibrator, but then I remembered how much you seemed to enjoy eggs when we had breakfast together at the beach."

"I do love eggs." She smiled sheepishly, still studying the toy. "How do you use this?"

My face lit up and my cock jumped. The fun was about to begin. "Well, there are lots of ways you can play with this . . . you can stick it up your pussy or stick it in your butt."

"My butt?" Her voice rose an octave.

I gave her a chaste kiss on top of her head. "Don't worry. That's for later. Right now, I'm going to show you how to stimulate yourself with it." I removed the wireless remote control and a tube of lube from the box. Whoo hoo! We were going to get to play together. I loved anything with batteries.

I squirted a generous amount of lube on the smooth surface of the little egg, and then decided I wanted a better view of watching Jen play with it. I wanted to see her tight little pussy and watch the expression on her face when she found her clit and made herself come.

Not wasting a second, I swept down the coverlet. Man, she was adorable in her fuzzy Santa print pajamas; they were so cute on her I almost hated what I was about to do next. *Say good-bye to your PJs, baby.* In one swift move, I tore off her bottoms and tossed them onto the shaggy pink carpet. And then with the remote in my hand, I crawled to the edge of the bed.

"What the hell did you just do? These were my favorite pajamas!"

"I'll buy you a new pair," I replied, spreading her bare legs. "Now, bend your knees and put the egg on your clit. It's playtime."

Holding the little egg between her index finger and thumb, she hesitantly put the toy between her legs right where I wanted it. I flicked on the remote and adjusted the setting to the pulsating sensation. At the sound of the buzz, her body jumped from the unexpected vibration.

"Oh my God," she squeed.

"Shhh!" I made a silencing gesture, placing my index finger over my mouth. "You don't want to wake your parents up."

"Right," she murmured.

"Now, move it around. Experiment."

She got braver with the egg, running it up and down

her slick folds. *My* playground. Little oohs and aahs spilled from her lips. Christ. Her pussy was exquisite. The delicate folds so pink and wet. My cock swelled beneath the fabric of my pajama bottoms at the sight of it, but she didn't notice the rising tent between my legs because her eyes were squeezed shut. She moaned with the pleasure she was giving herself . . . and me. I might not be able to wait for her to come. Damn. That would be a shame.

She found her clit again and started making ragged little circles around it—the way a child colored in an object with a crayon. Her back arched and her breathing grew harsh.

"Oh my God," she cried out again, her pretty face contorting.

Fuck. I hope she wasn't going to wake her parents up. That would be bad.

"Do you like your new toy?" I asked in an effort to distract her.

She nodded zealously. "Yes!"

"Do I get a thank you?"

"Thank you." She choked out the words.

"You're welcome." It was time to turn it up a notch. I flipped the switch to a higher speed.

She shrieked with ecstasy. "What did you just do?" she moaned upon the change in tempo.

"It's such a fun toy," I retorted, watching her writhe with tortuous pleasure. My cock was so hard I thought it would burst through my pajamas.

Whimpers. "I'm going to come!" she cried as softly as she could which wasn't softly at all.

The words I wanted to hear. She bit down hard on her quivering lip and squeezed her eyes tighter, tears leaking out the corners. I clutched my dick as her whole body shook with spasms of pleasure. Her head fell back against the headboard as she rode her orgasm out.

She was a sight to behold. Her body glistening and her face impassioned. A fallen angel. Mine to love.

"Hey."

Slowly, she lifted her head and blinked open her eyes. She held me in her gaze before breathing one word: "Fuck."

My favorite word in the world. It was my turn to play with her. My cock was going to detonate if it didn't get inside her soon.

"My turn." I frantically pulled off my drawstring pajama bottoms and freed my swollen, aching, hard-as-rock cock. Dropping the remote onto the bed, I crawled to her on my knees until I was positioned right between her splayed legs with my cock aimed at her shimmering pussy. Still clutching the buzzing egg, she looked at me, her eyes lustful and her mouth parted as if she was holding her breath in sweet anticipation of my next move.

"I'm going to fuck your brains out, tiger, but I want you to play with yourself with the egg while I do."

She nodded feverishly. Without wasting a second, I drew her closer to me and plunged my cock inside her. It glided in effortlessly, her pussy so wet and ready. "Oh, tiger," I groaned, "you feel fucking incredible." On my next breath, I was banging her ruthlessly.

As moans gathered in the back of her throat, I tore off her pajama top, craving her raw silky flesh against mine. I circled my arms around her slender torso and felt the sweet friction of her puckered nipples against my chest as she rocked with me and clenched my cock with her muscles. She'd gotten used to my size. My cock pulsated while heat coiled between my thighs. Fuck. I wasn't going to last long.

"Play with the egg," I breathed against her neck. She nodded and I could feel her hand move back between her legs. The buzzing echoed in my ears.

"Blake, I'm going to explode," she screamed, digging the nails of her free hand into my bicep.

I quickly smashed my lips on hers to smother her sounds before she woke up not only her parents, but the entire neighborhood. This girl was one hell of a screamer.

On a deep thrust, my climax surged forward and I squeezed her tightly against me. "Eyes, tiger!" I wanted her to watch me come.

As her eyes pried open, I combusted, my hot release shooting out as she shuddered all around my pulsing cock. To stifle my own loud sounds, I bit down on her shoulder, close to her arched neck, for sure leaving a mark, if not a tear. I'd always wanted to bite her and now I had.

Wasted, I collapsed against her, my head falling onto her marked shoulder. She ruffled my damp hair with one hand and caressed my sweat-laced back with other. It felt so good. She felt so good.

"I love you, tiger," I rasped against her sweet glistening skin. How easy these once unspoken words now came to me. I loved her so fucking much.

She nuzzled my neck before taking my mouth in hers. "Blake, you're a very naughty boy."

Indeed I was. Blake Burns was a *very* naughty boy. But Santa had looked the other way and given me just what I wanted for Christmas.

Chapter 4

Jennifer

The egg was a wonder toy. Blake showed me every which way to use it—from stimulating his cock to putting it in my butt while he fucked me. The sensation of having it in my butt was beyond words. I experienced an out of this world orgasm that made me see stars. And there were more levels of stimulation. One called escalation—vibrations that started at a slow speed, then sped up and then stopped abruptly making me desperate for more, and another called surging, a mixture of pulsation and normal vibrating. I swear, I don't know how many times we fucked. And I swear, I don't know how either of us didn't wake my parents up.

Blake wanted me to go to sleep with the egg inside me so I would wake up wet and stimulated, ready for him. I told him that wasn't necessary. Just having him in my bed, naked and raw, was all I needed. But he insisted, and I finally gave in, not having the energy to fight him. We exchanged yet another round of "I love you." I'd lost count of how many times I'd said those words. And heard them. But I couldn't get enough. In no time, I fell asleep in his arms, cradled in his warm manly body.

I was the first to awaken in the morning. My eyes fluttered open as awareness seeped into my brain. I was still spooned in Blake and could feel his heart beating against my back. One sculpted arm curled above my head while the other draped over my tummy. We had fallen asleep in this position, flesh to flesh, his erection pressed tightly against my backside. I twisted my neck to peer at him. God, he was beautiful in the morning. Soft breaths, as soothing as a cat's purr, emanated from his gently parted lips, and a lock of silky hair fell onto his forehead. The fine layer of stubble that circled his jaw made him even sexier than imaginable. Oh God. What had I done to deserve this man? *This* God. This man who loved me and whom I loved back with my heart and soul. Usually, I woke up on Christmas morning with excitement and anticipation. Today, I woke up totally contented and satisfied. Santa had come and dropped off my best present ever. Blake Burns. *Thank you, Santa.*

The familiar sounds of Christmas morning sounded in my ears. Downstairs, I could hear "Deck the Halls" playing on my parents' stereo system (they still hadn't upgraded to surround sound). When I was a little girl, I was always the first to wake up and trot downstairs, eager to see what Santa had brought me. As I grew older and learned Santa = Dad, I slept later, needing the extra hours of sleep to supplement my time-sucking hormones. I could have stayed in bed all day with Blake—just like this in his arms—but that wasn't an option. As sunlight filtered into my room, I remembered something. Before we'd fallen asleep, Blake had told me Santa had another surprise for me—another toy. While nothing could possibly top that fucking (no pun intended) egg, I was suddenly eager to find out what it was.

I maneuvered myself so I was facing Blake. I kissed his forehead, and his dazzling blue eyes blinked open.

"Merry Christmas, Blake." I brushed the wisp of hair off his forehead. My beautiful bedhead!

He smiled and his eyes twinkled like stars. "Merry Christmas, tiger." He traced my jaw with his fingertips before smacking his lips against mine. Another all-consuming, tongue-driven kiss ensued. I could easily get used to waking up this way every morning.

After taking separate showers (we couldn't risk taking one together with my parents up), we got dressed, both of us in jeans and sweaters. I was also wearing something else at Blake's insistence—the little vibrating egg in my pussy. At the moment, it wasn't vibrating. Blake had set the remote to the "off" position.

"You'd better behave," I whispered as we headed downstairs.

"Don't worry."

"Promise?"

"Promise." He playfully slapped my ass.

I worried Blake wouldn't be true to his word. He was a very naughty boy. My parents had learned over dinner we worked together but had no clue he was more than just a friend or that I worked for him. At a porn channel no less. Though Mom and Dad knew the job with Peanuts, Conquest Broadcasting's former children's network, had fallen through, I'd led them to believe I was working for another division of the company. I'd just conveniently failed to mention it was Adult Entertainment.

When we got downstairs, "I'm Dreaming of a White Christmas" was playing, and my dad was in the living room in his favorite reclining chair, reading the morning paper over a cup of coffee.

"Good morning, you two sleepyheads," he said, looking up from his paper and smiling.

"Good morning," Blake and I responded in unison.

"You two sleep well?"

Blake grinned. "The best bed I've ever slept in."

I cringed. Why did everything this man say have to be loaded with sexual innuendo? I sure as hell didn't want my parents to know he'd fucked my brains out right under our roof. Before I could respond, my mother waltzed into the room, holding two mugs of steaming coffee.

"I could hear you two come downstairs from the kitchen. I've brought you some fresh coffee."

"Thanks, Mom," I said, taking the mugs from her. I handed one to Blake.

Mom: "Blake, I hope you take cream in yours."

"Yes, thank you, Mrs. McCoy. The more cream the better."

I almost regurgitated my first sip of coffee. Last night, while he was fucking me for the second time, Blake had told me that he was going to cream me as he was about to come. My pussy quivered.

My father rose from his chair and ambled toward our Christmas tree. "Now that everyone's up, let's see what Santa's brought."

The rest of us followed him. As we gathered around the tree, my mother apologized to Blake. "Blake, dear, had we known you'd be here with us, we would have surely gotten you something. I feel terrible."

Blake smiled warmly at my mother. "No worries. Being here with you and your husband . . . and Jennifer . . . is more than I could possibly ask for."

Upon saying my name, he shot me a sexy little wink. It sent tingles down my spine. The sooner we opened presents, the better. He was affecting me again.

As was tradition in our house, we all sat down around the tree, with our mugs of coffee, and began the ritual. Cross-legged, Blake sat right next to me. So close, I could feel the heat of his body. My heart pitter-pattered, and my pussy felt as lit up as the Christmas tree.

My parents and I exchanged gifts first. They were thrilled with what I'd gotten them—matching lambswool scarves and each a book—and I was equally delighted with what they'd gotten me—a stunning Coach backpack that matched my briefcase. It was quite an extravagant present given they were now living on my retired father's pension. I gave them each a big hug.

Blake and I watched as my parents then exchanged gifts. After all these years of marriage, a deep-rooted, true love still lit up their eyes as they handed each other festively wrapped up boxes. For Mom, a lovely red pullover sweater, and for Dad, a handsome argyle cardigan. Every year, the same glow, the same thank you, the same kiss on the cheek. Knowing my best friend Libby's parents had gone through an ugly divorce, I felt blessed to have my loving parents.

There were three remaining large boxes. All from Blake.

"Those two are for you, Mr. and Mrs. McCoy," he said, pointing to the two monstrous side by side boxes, identical in size and wrapped in exactly the same hunter green paper. Each was topped off with a humongous red velvet bow.

"You didn't have to buy us anything," said my mother, reaching for the two boxes and handing one to my father. I watched as they opened them and gawked when they uncovered what was inside. Two magnificent Ralph Lauren plaid cashmere blankets. They must have cost a fortune. My parents could never afford anything like them.

Blake was beaming. "I hope you like them. My parents have the same ones, so I thought they were a good bet."

My mother lovingly held the soft cashmere blanket to her cheekbone and then wrapped it around her shoulders. "Oh Blake, dear. They're so beautiful. You shouldn't have."

"My pleasure."

"An outstanding choice, son. Thank you from both of us." My father, though he didn't blatantly show it, was equally impressed and delighted with Blake's extravagant gift.

Blake gathered the last remaining box in his hands. This box was different in size and shape than my parents'—big and bulky—and it was wrapped in a whimsical, childlike snowman-themed paper. "This is for you, tiger."

My stomach muscles twisted. Shit. He called me "tiger" in front of my parents. While my mother, enraptured with her new blanket, was oblivious, my father raised a brow. Maybe, he just thought it was odd.

"Thank you," I stammered, taking the box from him. It was not particularly heavy or solid. I had no idea what could be inside. I carefully unwrapped it. A big, red shiny box was now in my lap. Slowly, I lifted off the lid.

My breath hitched in my throat when I eyed what was inside. With trembling hands, I took it out of the box. Another toy. This time a beautiful, white plush tiger with black stripes, a pink nose, and glass eyes as green as mine. About three feet tall, it was in a seated position, its limbs spread apart as if ready for a hug and then a fuck. Around its neck hung an exquisite pink tourmaline heart on a gold chain. My birthstone! I had told him in Vegas my birthday was in October. He remembered! My own heart hammered as my eyes met Blake's. I knew this necklace was meant for me to wear. To have his heart close to mine.

"Do you like it?" he asked, his voice soft and sultry. "It's a snow tiger. They're an endangered species. Very special and rare."

"I love it!" Tears were verging. *I love you.*

So wanting to hug him, to be in his arms, I hugged the cuddly tiger instead. "Thank you," I said in almost a whisper, pressing my lips against its soft, sweet face. A tear escaped my eye and disappeared into the tiger's velvety fur.

My mother's voice brought me out of my trance-like state. "Honey, do you want to help me make breakfast?"

I lifted my head, hoping tears were no longer falling. "Sure, Mom."

"Wonderful. I'm making eggs." *Eggs?* She turned to Blake. "Blake dear, how do you like your eggs?"

Blake shot me a cocky grin and then responded. "Mrs. McCoy, I'm easy. I like my eggs every which way."

My pussy throbbed. Oh, God, egg talk! I suddenly became aware again of the little egg hiding inside me.

My father stood up. "While my girls make breakfast, I'm going to dig out the driveway."

I glanced out the window. Our front yard was covered in snow. At least three feet—significantly more if you counted the drifts against our almost buried picket fence.

"Let me do it," insisted Blake.

My father smiled. "I could use the exercise. But I'd appreciate your help, son."

"You've got it, Mr. McCoy."

My father nodded. "Thank you, and you can call me Harold."

As my mother and I retreated to the kitchen, Dad and Blake readied for the manly task that awaited them.

Chapter 5

Blake

While I was in extraordinarily good shape from working out at the gym and doing the Santa Monica Stairs, I'd never shoveled snow before. At our family house in Aspen that we'd recently sold for a small fortune, we always had plows come by to dig us out. Man, shoveling snow was fucking hard work. I was breathing heavily and working up a sweat despite the nippy temperature. As I struggled to scoop up the dense powder from the packed driveway, I watched in awe as Jen's father seemed to effortlessly shovel it away.

"Pace yourself," he urged. "And use your shoulder muscles as much as possible so you don't hurt your back."

He was definitely in good shape for a man his age, and I tried my dammedest to keep up with him. Like with pumping weights or any sport, my mind was filled with the task at hand. But when I took short little breaks, my mind drifted to Jennifer.

I'd had the most sensual experience of my life last night. Watching her play with her toy and come over and over again was one thing. But sleeping with her in the raw in my arms was something else. Our naked bodies spooned together, almost one, her heart mine, palmed in my hand. Sharing a blanket, our bodies warming each other. Yes, I had fucked many women, but I'd never slept with one after the act. Only my tiger. The girl I loved.

I could have spent the whole day with her in bed, fucking and snuggling, but that wasn't going to happen at her parents' house. Plus, I woke up excited about giving my girl her other Christmas present. My heart pounded with anticipation as she unwrapped it under the tree and then exploded with elation when I saw in her eyes how much she loved the plush tiger. I was lucky to have found it at a toy shop in Ketchum and the tourmaline heart in a nearby jewelry store. Buying a woman presents was something new to me too. I never did that; all they got from me was my cock. But when it came to Jennifer McCoy, I couldn't buy her enough. That's how much I loved her. I could have easily gone into every store and bought her a boatload of beautiful things, but the reality of that badass blizzard combined with my burning urge to see her stopped me. Buying something for her—especially something perfect—gave me a high like a drug. I'd experienced this very high when I'd purchased the painting. It took my breath away—almost as much as she did. I couldn't wait to fasten the pendant necklace around her neck. Wherever she was, my heart would always be near hers.

Little by little, we cleared the snow and could even start to see the pavement. Mr. McCoy gave me another helpful tip—to keep one hand close to the shovel blade for better leverage. I readjusted my hands and discovered he was right again. It was easier this way.

We worked away in silence for another half hour. Heated up, I peeled off my jacket and wrapped it around my waist.

The silence was unexpectedly broken by Mr. McCoy.

"Blake, I googled you this morning."

I gulped and felt my face flare. I speared my shovel into a pile of snow and met his intense eyes with mine.

"So you head up SIN-TV. That's a porn channel. Right, son?"

"Yes, sir, it is." There was no pussyfooting around the truth. He knew.

"I assume my daughter works for you. In the porn industry?"

My throat tightened. I swallowed painfully. "Yes, sir. She does. She's wonderful at her job." It had quickly become apparent to me Jen had never told her overprotective parents about her real job. They probably thought she worked in children's television. For sure, they didn't know about the Don Springer incident, and I was going to keep it that way.

"What exactly does she do?" ventured Harold.

"It's not what you think. She doesn't handle the rowdy stuff."

His brows shot up. "What does that mean?"

"She's a development executive. She's developing a really classy block based on bestselling books targeted to women."

"You mean like that *Fifty Shades* book?"

By this time, who hadn't heard about that book? "Yes, but even better." I'd actually read a few and was quite impressed by the storylines, character development, and overall writing. And the level of steaminess was off the charts.

"What I'm thinking of doing is making these productions not only for women but by women. Women writers, producers, and directors." I hadn't yet shared this thought with Jennifer, but was positive she would jump all over it.

After another shovel of snow, Harold nodded his head approvingly. "That's a good idea. She seems so happy, and she's told us how much she loves her job though she never told us she was involved with adult entertainment. My wife doesn't know, but eventually I'll tell her."

"Thanks," I said, not knowing what else to say.

Harold and I both shoveled more snow. We were almost finished.

"One last thing, son."

The tone of his voice made me uneasy.

"I saw you with my daughter last night."

My stomach knotted. I put my shovel down. "What do you mean?"

"You know what I mean. You kissed her."

Words stayed tangled in my lumpy throat. My face flushed. I couldn't hide the truth.

"You're more than just her boss. She's in love with you."

I sucked in a breath of the cold air and shot out the words. "And, Mr. McCoy, I'm in love with her."

To my surprise and relief, he smiled. "Did you have anything to do with her breakup with Bradley?"

"No, nothing at all." A lie as white as snow. I wiped some sweat off my brow and inwardly shuddered.

"Well, to be honest with you, son, I never liked him though I never told my daughter or my wife that. He just rubbed me the wrong way." He regarded me warmly, his eyes squinting from the glint of the snow and the sun. "I have a good feeling about you, Blake. Take good care of my little girl, Jennie. She's my one and only."

I smiled back at him. "I will, sir."

His eyes darkened. "And make sure you don't hurt her."

I nodded. "You have my word."

Satisfied with my response, he tossed his shovel. "C'mon, let's head back inside. I'm as hungry as a bear."

Equally famished, I followed suit. Warmth radiated inside me. I'd scored points with Jennifer's father. When I got back to LA, I was going to have a heart-to-heart with my dad too. Especially since Jen and I worked together, he needed to know.

Chapter 6

Jennifer

I helped my mom make breakfast in our charming knotty-pine kitchen. Despite the fact she was a gourmet cook, she'd never updated it. It still bore memories of my childhood. We were standing a shoulder's width apart, working away at a Formica counter.

I took a break from the fruit I was dicing. "Mom, can I ask you a question?"

Beating eggs in a bowl, she smiled at me. "Of course, honey. Anything."

"How did you know you loved Dad?"

Her smile morphed into a concerned frown. "Oh dear, you're still in love with Bradley?" She'd clearly not picked up on my feelings toward Blake. Though so much of me wanted to share what was going on, it was all too new, and I was unsure how things would move forward once we were back at work. I responded with a sigh.

"Hardly. I'm totally over him. I'm just curious. That's all."

My mom quirked a relieved smile. "I fell in love with him the minute I saw him. I couldn't stop thinking about him."

My mom had been his student his first year as a young assistant professor of English at Boise State. There was only a year difference in age between them.

"And then what?"

"The feeling was mutual. He asked me out."

"Weren't you nervous about going out with your professor?" When I thought about it, a student-professor relationship was not that different from an employee-boss one.

"Yes. I was. But my heart ruled my brain. I was young."

I was young too. But I knew what'd happened. Ultimately, that one date turned into a relationship. A love affair. A jealous female student made the university aware of their relationship. Fraternization was not allowed. My mother, an aspiring scholar, sacrificed her career, putting my father's interests and needs before hers. She left the university, and three months later she and my father married. While I was crazy in love with my boss, there were so many doubts circling my head. Conquest Broadcasting didn't forbid work relationships, but it wasn't going to be easy. And it wouldn't surprise me if one of his jealous blond bimbos like Kitty-Kat did me in. Both my career and my heart were at stake. I needed to know.

"Mom, do you have any regrets?"

She smiled wistfully. "Not one. Your father and I were meant to be. I couldn't imagine life without him." She paused and pecked my cheek. "And you, my darling, were meant to be ours."

I hugged my mom, at once excited and anxious about what the future might bring. Perhaps, Blake and I could find some time to talk. There was a lot to talk about.

I helped my mom serve the beautiful platter of scrambled eggs she'd made along with the linked sausages and a large bowl of fruit salad. Buttered toast, fresh squeezed orange juice, and fresh coffee were also on the breakfast menu. I was never going to be as good a cook or hostess as my mom. Somehow, that Martha Stewart gene had skipped me.

Blake and Dad were already at the kitchen table. Both were rosy-cheeked from being outdoors. The color in Blake's face made him even sexier to me. His eyes sparkled.

"That looks delicious, Mrs. McCoy," Blake said as my mother handed him the platter.

My mother smiled at the compliment. "Thank you, dear. Help yourself and pass them around. And please call me Meg."

Once the other courses were on the round table, my mother and I joined them. I helped myself to a generous portion of everything though it was hard to eat with my beautiful Blake in my face.

He ate heartily. Something I found so sexy about him. "There's nothing like good old eggs and sausage for breakfast," he commented between bites.

So far, he'd been very well behaved. I kept waiting for him to trigger the vibrating egg, but maybe he'd forgotten about it. Relaxing a little, I lifted a forkful of the perfectly cooked eggs to my mouth. As I did, the shoulder of the oversized sweater I was wearing drooped down.

My mother's eyes widened. "Darling, what's that red welt on your shoulder?"

Flushing, I gulped down the eggs. I'd totally forgotten about Blake's bite. "Um, uh, I think it's a bug bite."

Mom's face grew alarmed. "Oh dear Lord, I hope we don't have bedbugs." She gazed at my Dad who wore a bemused expression. "Darling, we'd better call an exterminator right after the holidays."

"I don't think we'll have to."

My father winked at me. My stomach muscles tightened. What did he and Blake talk about outside? Did he know?

I shot Blake a glance, but he kept a straight poker face.

My still concerned mother asked if he'd gotten any

bites. "Not a one," he replied and went back to heartily eating his breakfast. I hastily pulled my sweater up over my shoulder. I'd lost my appetite.

My mom noticed I wasn't eating. "Jen, what's wrong? Why aren't you eating more?"

At that minute, Blake became Mr. Bad Boy. With the remote likely in his left hand under the table, he turned the vibrating egg on full speed. It pulsed inside my pussy. Holy shit! I couldn't sit still. My eyes locked on his. He grinned at me fiendishly.

"Jen, you really should have more of your mother's eggs. They're so delicious."

Yes, they were. Except there was another egg I was finding more delicious. The one buried inside me. The pulsing was driving me crazy. Taking me over the edge. I pressed my lips together so I wouldn't shriek. Then I began to hum, fearful my parents would hear my crotch buzzing.

"Jennifer, are sure you're okay?" Worry laced my mother's voice.

"Yes, Mom. I'm just really full." *Oh was I!* I was going to explode.

My orgasm began its takeover. I jumped up from my chair "I need to use the bathroom. I'll be right back."

On my way out of the kitchen, I shot Blake a dirty look. He'd promised to behave. I should have never trusted him. He grinned that devastating diabolic grin. I raced to the guest bathroom and let myself come with waves of pleasure.

"Beautiful bastard," I sighed as I pulled out the egg. He'd made me hunger for him all over again. I craved and loved him so much.

Chapter 7

Jennifer

By the time we finished breakfast and I helped my mom clear the table, it was close to noon. My parents lingered over coffee, telling Blake childhood stories about me. While I was grateful Blake wasn't forced to tell work-related stories, mortification raced through me. Blake, however, seemed to enjoy each and every one and frequently laughed out loud. God, he was sexy when he let out that deep laugh, his two little dimples lighting up his face. Even I had to laugh when my parents shared the time my father had told me I needed a little elbow grease to finish building my dollhouse. Silly me ran to my mother's pantry, yanked out the shortening, and smeared it all over my arms. What a doofgirl!

Shortly after breakfast, my father shrugged on his heavy alpaca coat. "We're going to visit the Joneses." It was a tradition. Every Christmas day for as long as I could remember, my parents stopped by their best friends' house for an exchange of presents and a little grog. Dad looked my way. I was seated on the living room couch next to Blake, cuddling my snow tiger. I longed to be cuddling him.

"Why don't you two kids relax and romp in the snow," he said, buttoning up his coat.

"Are you sure, Dad?" I asked as my mother joined him. She looked positively stunning in the cherry red wool coat she wore only on Christmas. The heavy snow boots on her feet only accentuated everything lovely above them.

"Of course, darling," chimed in my mother.

With a wink targeted at Blake, my dad told us to have fun.

It was the perfect first snow of the winter. Three feet deep and powdery. Our house—in fact, the entire street, looked like a Hallmark Christmas card—with the trees and rooftops dusted with a thick layer of the pearl white powder. The temperature was cold, but not unbearable, and the sun was shining brightly, creating a glare from the snow.

Bundled up in waterproof winter gear, Blake and I wasted no time frolicking in my backyard. I beat him to it and threw a snowball at him. I got him good in the chest.

"You're going to pay for that, McCoy," he growled. Wasting no time, he retaliated and got me hard in the ass as I tried to escape.

"That hurt," I giggled.

"Not as much as this one," he shouted back at me, throwing yet another ready-made one straight at me. Hah! This time I ducked behind a tree, and he missed.

Our snowball fight escalated until we were out of breath and doubled over with laughter. Blake wrapped his arms around me from behind and nuzzled the little exposed area of my scarf-shrouded neck. "Come on. Let's build a snowman."

"Cool." Crouching, I instantly formed a snowball and began packing it with snow. Blake squatted down and followed suit. Side by side, we rolled our snowballs across the dense white powder. In no time, we built three giant but different sized snowballs as well as built up a sweat beneath our heavy clothes. Blake stacked the three weighty balls, one on top of the other. I scouted the yard for anything we could use to make a face—coming up with a few chunks of coal and twigs for his arms. Blake topped him off with his silly reindeer hat, stretching it over Mr. Snowman's head until it almost ripped. I couldn't stop laughing.

"Too bad we don't have a carrot for his nose," I snorted through my tears of laughter.

"Too bad we don't have a cucumber for his dick," laughed my companion. I laughed harder, so hard my face hurt.

And then, without warning, Blake collapsed onto

the snow-covered ground, flat on his back with his arms outstretched. His eyes were glued shut.

"Blake!" Panic gripped me. Maybe he'd had a heart attack or something. All that shoveling and those heavy snowballs. Ridden with guilt and despair, I fell to my knees beside him. My fingers raked his hair. "Blake, Blake, are you okay? Please be okay."

There was no response. Oh, God. He was going to die in my backyard. If he died, a part of me died too. At that moment, I realized how much I really, *really* loved him.

"Blake," I pleaded again, "please open your eyes. I love you so much." A tear fell onto his lips. I pressed my lips against his and kissed it away. Oh, God. Was this going to be the last time his soft lips touched mine?

Then suddenly, magically, just like in Snow White, his eyes fluttered open. The power of a kiss! "Gotcha!" he laughed.

I didn't know whether to laugh or cry. I was at once relieved and furious with him.

"That wasn't funny," I scoffed, tossing a handful of snow at him.

I still wasn't over his little prank when he began to repeatedly open and close his arms and legs in tandem. It was if he was doing jumping jacks lying down in the snow.

"What are you doing, you crazy man?"

"Seriously? I'm making a snow angel. Don't tell me

you've never made one."

"Are you kidding? My parents would never let me lie down in the snow."

"Come. Let's make one together. Get on top of me."

Hesitantly, I did as bid, positioning my body so my arms and legs were directly on his outstretched ones. My chin rested on his chest, and even beneath his heavy down jacket, I could feel his heart beat for me.

"Perfect. Now just follow my movements." He began to scissor his arms and legs again, and as he opened and closed them, I did the same with mine. Wow! This was fun.

As we got into a rhythm, it was more than just his heartbeat I felt. Beneath my torso, I could feel an erection pressing into me. His cock was hardening and swelling. Holy shit!

"Having you on me this way is giving me a fucking hard-on. Tiger, let's show this dickless snowman what he's *really* missing."

My eyes grew as round as saucers. "You want to fuck in the snow?"

"Yep."

"You'll freeze your ass off."

"No, I'll *fucking* freeze my ass off. Now, pull down your pants."

Raising myself a little, I managed to somehow to slide my snow pants—and my tights—down enough to give him entry. The cold air stung my buttocks.

His arms and legs continued to slice the snow. "Now, pull down my fly and put my cock inside you."

With one hand, I reached into the tight space between us and did as he asked. Holy cow! He'd gone Commando. I could feel the heat of his cock through my gloves, and as I inserted it into me, its hotness contrasted sharply to the coldness of the air. I moaned into his chest.

"Oh, baby, you're like a fucking oven," he breathed as he filled me to the hilt.

I moved my arms back onto his, and we went back to making our snow angel, opening and closing our limbs, wider and faster, as he pounded into me, keeping pace. Harder and deeper. Faster and faster. The melody of "Jingle Bells" echoed in my head. *Oh what fun, it is to ride your cock in the deep white snow and play.*

Despite the frigid temperature, my body was heating up. I could feel sweat beading on my skin beneath my heavy clothes. My chin rested on his chest and I gazed up at him. The expression on his glowing face was one of pure ecstasy. My fingers clasped his wrists like manacles so I wouldn't fall off, and my legs pressed firmly against his powerful muscular thighs. I was sure we were melting the snow.

"Oh, tiger," he groaned. "I'm so fucking close to coming."

"Me too," I moaned. The pulsing in my core rose to a feverish pitch. I was like a volcano ready to erupt. I roared his name as I climaxed around him. Waves of white bliss, as blinding as the snow, spiraled through me. In a breath, I felt him jolt with his own volcanic eruption, his hot molten lava pouring into me.

I rested my head against his chest for a few long minutes until our breathing calmed down. My stinging, frozen ass brought awareness back to me.

"Blake, that was amazing."

He blew out of puff of air. "Yeah, fucking amazing." A boyish dimpled grin lit up his handsome face. "Come on, tiger, let's see how our snow angel turned out. We may have fucked it up."

Giggling at his double entendre, I got into a squatting position between his spread out, V'd legs. Definitely not my most graceful move. He sat up and then helped me stand up with him. As I pulled my snow pants and tights up over my butt, I watched as he tucked his spent dick into his pants and zipped up his fly. Snow pants were not the most flattering things to wear, but on him, they looked sinfully sexy because I knew what was beneath.

"Look!" A warm smile spread across his face as his vision took in our creation. "I'm going to take a picture." He whipped out his ubiquitous iPhone from a jacket pocket while I stared at the snow angel we'd created together in awe.

"Oh my God!" I rasped. Where our arms had flapped madly, there were wings, and below, a bell-

shaped gown was etched in the snow from the move-
ment of our legs. To my utter amazement, around the
imprint of our heads, the sun cast a halo. Our beautiful
angel! Heaven on Earth! Magic! Pure magic! Tears
spilled from my eyes.

"Don't cry on me again," whispered Blake, removing a glove to wipe them away.

"I can't help it," I sniffed. "An angel is watching
us."

"*You* are my angel." And with that, he crashed
down on my mouth with a hot, passionate kiss while
Mr. Snowman looked on with envy.

Chapter 8

Blake

We warmed each other up by taking a hot bath together. Jennifer sat between my legs, her back toward me. Happy to see the necklace I'd given her around her neck, I intermittently sponged her and covered her with kisses. But something was weighing on my mind.

"Jen, I didn't use a condom outside."

"I know."

"It's the first time I've never used one. I should have told you I've been tested and asked if you were on birth control."

"I am."

I inwardly sighed with relief and nuzzled her neck. She lifted her ponytail to give me better access.

"Blake, I've never had sex without a condom either."

So, we had shared firsts. Sex with Jennifer was incredible. I didn't think it could get better. Fucking her in the snow was the best sex I'd ever had. I could still feel her raw warmth against my own heated rawness.

The feeling of spilling into her and feeling her pussy throb all around me had sent me flying to the moon. My cock swelled at the sweet memory. Pulling her tight against me, I wondered—had it been as good for her as it was for me?

One word from her mouth gave me my answer. "Again."

After our mind-blowing tub sex, we dressed in jeans and sweaters and headed downstairs. Jen made us lunch—ham and cheese sandwiches—and we cuddled up together on the living room couch to watch some TV.

"Oh, Blake! The SpongeBob Christmas episode is on," she squeed after channel surfing.

I remembered her mentioning at my parents' Shabbat dinner that *SpongeBob SquarePants* was her favorite cartoon. It had become apparent to me she was obsessed with this animated dude. She'd even written her master's thesis on him. On his sexual appeal of all things. As stupid as this may sound, I was jealous of some dumbass cartoon character. *What does he have that I don't?* I needed to know.

"Why do you like SpongeBob so much? I mean, he's a total spineless geek who looks like a wedge of Swiss cheese on legs. He probably doesn't even have a dick."

She hit me with a pillow. "Don't talk about SpongeBob that way. He's funny, sweet, and innocent. And has a big heart. He always sees the good in people despite their faults. He's a virgin, holding out for the right woman. His Sandy. That's what makes him appealing. Give him a chance, Mr. Burns."

Thirty laugh-out-loud minutes later, I was a SpongeBob convert. Call me gay. I loved the goofy little guy. But I loved my little tiger now even more as if more was possible. Had I not been afraid of her parents bursting through the front door, I would have fucked her senseless on the couch and smothered her with kisses.

After watching the cartoon, Jennifer had an idea. She wanted to give me a mini-tour of Boise. Taking my Jeep, we passed by Boise State where her dad had taught and then headed downtown. After enthusiastically pointing out various sites, Jen grew pensive.

I lowered the sound of the radio and asked, "What are you thinking about, tiger?"

She twitched a half-smile. "You."

I smiled back and tugged at her adorable knit cap. "That's always a good thing."

"I'm not sure."

"What do you mean?" My voice was edgy. Fuck. Was she having doubts about our relationship?

"I'm worried about how we're going to handle

things. We work together. You're my boss. And there's no way I can keep it a secret from my roommate Libby, who has the biggest mouth in the world."

I chewed my lip. To be honest, I hadn't give much thought to the future. Except she was in it. She had a point. We needed to figure out how to handle the situation at work. I'd never had an office affair. And this was beyond an affair.

After much deliberation, I responded. "I'm going to talk to my father. He'll know what to do."

Jennifer nodded. "That's a good idea. I guess I'll tell Libby."

I wasn't too crazy about her tell-Libby-tell-the-world friend. She was such a know-it-all. "How do you think she'll react?"

To my utter surprise, Jen burst out laughing. "Not too well. She thinks you're a self-centered, arrogant asshole."

"Screw her." My blood was boiling. "She doesn't know me the way you do."

Her laughter deepened. "For your information, Mr. Burns, you actually can be a self-centered, arrogant asshole but—"

Before she could finish her sentence, I pulled off the road with a screech.

"You're pissing me off."

She was not the least bit intimidated. "You didn't let me finish my sentence."

My forehead creased as her face softened.

"I was going to say: but I love you so much anyway. Now get over here." Grabbing the edges of my scarf, she yanked me toward her. Her lips went down on mine with a wild, spontaneous kiss that she deepened with her tongue. She tasted like warm sugar. So, so good. We moaned into each other's mouths. The little tease rubbed my cock. It stirred beneath the denim of my jeans and grew rigid. Fuck. I needed her to give me head. Desperately.

Just as I reached for my fly, there was a loud rapping on my passenger door window. I abruptly pulled away from Jen. Able to see who was outside the door, she pressed her lips together as if she was stifling laughter. I pivoted my head and could feel my face turn candy-cane red. Balls. It was a cop. I thought they didn't work on Christmas. I quickly lowered my window.

"Hello, officer," I said with as much coolness as I could muster.

He furrowed his brows. "Is there a problem here?"

"N-no," I stuttered. Bullshit. There was a problem. A biggie. My cock and balls were fucking killing me.

He flashed a crooked smile. "Good. Then, I'll be on my way. Merry Christmas."

"Merry Christmas, officer." *Asswipe.*

The cop sped off in his patrol car and I turned to face Jennifer. She had her hand clasped over her mouth and then burst into another clap of laughter. She was laughing so hard she was crying.

"That wasn't funny," I grumbled.

"It was!" She could barely get the words out.

Fuming, I drew her close to me by her scarf. "You owe me a blow job."

Still laughing, her watering eyes lit up like lanterns. "I'll think about it."

Man, she was pissing me off more. I was quickly learning my tiger was a feisty one. I might have to tame her. Well, at least, I had something to look forward to.

She held my gaze in hers. That little dimpled smile curled on her upturned lips. Fuck, she was beautiful. Unable to resist, I smacked my lips one more time against hers and took off.

There wasn't much to do in downtown Boise. Being Christmas Day, virtually everything was closed. The one thing we could do was go to the movies. I wanted to see *The Wolf of Wall Street* with Leonardo DiCaprio; she wanted to see *Frozen*. A fucking Disney cartoon. Guess who won? Wrong. She did. I was giving into her every need and whim. I was seriously in love with her.

The theater was packed with parents and kids. Holding hands, we scanned the dozens of rows for two seats together. I took in the crowd and wondered—

would this be us in a few years? A married couple taking their kids to a movie on Christmas Day. A passing woman holding a toddler made me think of the day Jennifer and I had lunch with my pal Jaime and his twins. She was great with those babies. I turned to look at her. Yeah. She was going to make one damn good mother, and our babies were going to be fucking perfect.

We finally found two seats in the very back of the theater bordering the aisle. I told Jennifer to save my seat while I went to the concession stand to get some popcorn and Cokes. It'd been a long time since I'd been on a movie date with a girl. That's not what I did with hook-ups, who only escorted me to glamorous premiers.

The concession lines were long, filled with irritated parents and whiny kids. As I impatiently waited my turn, a funny thought crossed my mind. I bet cheapskate Dickwick made her buy her own popcorn and soda. And probably her movie ticket too. I snickered silently. Those days were over. Ancient history.

When I got back inside the theater, the movie had just started. The lights were down and the opening title sequence was playing. I lowered myself to the seat on the aisle and handed Jennifer a Coke. "Thanks," she whispered, her eyes glued to the big screen.

I held the big tub of popcorn in my lap and nibbled on some kernels. My mind was distracted. What the fuck did you do with a girl at the movies? Vague recollections of my junior high school days came back. You held her hand. And at some point, you made out with her. And if you were really lucky, you got a hand job and came home with some pussy on your pinky.

Okay. So, I held her hand. It was soft and warm. She didn't resist. So far so good. She reached into the bucket of popcorn and grabbed a handful. I watched as she popped one kernel at time into her mouth. She reached for another handful. And then another. Balls. It was going to be hard to make out with her if she was going to be eating popcorn the whole time.

Despite myself, I actually found myself getting into the movie. It was about this feisty girl who reminded me a lot of Jennifer and featured this hilarious snowman named Olaf that made me think of the one we'd built earlier in the day. And the CGI animation was pretty amazing. Cartoons had come a long way since *Mickey Mouse*.

In the middle of the movie, I heard Jennifer sniffling. I turned to look at her and tears were streaming down her cheeks. The song "Let It Go" was playing. Sung by the conflicted princess sister, it was about her adventurous journey of finding herself and letting go of the past.

"What's the matter, baby?" I whispered in Jen's ear.

She squeezed my hand and met my gaze. It was the first time her eyes had left the screen.

"Blake, would you tell me you love me again and kiss me?"

My heart melted like chocolate. I cradled her face in my hands and gave her the kind of kiss you only saw in movies. A lingering mixture of hard and soft. Sensuous and rough. Our cheeks touched and her hot tears heated my face. Our lips fit perfectly together. The lyrics of the song sounded in my head. There was no going back for my tiger. And there was no going back for me. The past was in the past.

The movie ended and the lights came back on. The theater emptied. But neither Jennifer nor I moved. Our mouths were locked. I was still kissing my brave, complicated tiger.

An usher's voice asking us to leave finally forced me to pull away. I gazed at Jen's beautiful tear-streaked face, and though I had a serious boner, she was all that mattered to me.

Still cupping her face in my hands, I said the words she needed to hear. "I love you, Jennifer McCoy."

She smiled.

When we got back to Jennifer's house, her parents were back from their afternoon visit with the Joneses. It was a little after four. Jen's father was in his favorite chair, reading the Shakespeare anthology Jennifer had given him for Christmas. I was pleased to see the cashmere blanket I'd bought draped over his legs.

The fireplace was crackling, and the air smelled sweet and delicious. Mrs. McCoy must be baking something. She was one hell of a cook.

"Hi, Dad," Jennifer said brightly as we headed into the living room. We'd left our outerwear and snowy boots in the entryway.

Harold looked up from his book. He lifted his reading glasses onto his head, and a warm smile spread on his face. "You kids have a fun this afternoon?"

Twinkly-eyed Jennifer told him she'd taken me on a tour of Boise and to see a movie.

"Which one?"

Before either of us could answer, Mrs. McCoy waltzed into the living room. She was wearing a floral apron and holding a tray with a platter of cookies and two mugs on it. The delicious aroma wafted in the air.

"I baked chocolate chip cookies and made some hot chocolate," she said with a big smile. She set the tray down on the large coffee table in front of the couch.

"Oh, Blake. You must have one of my mother's cookies. They're the best in the world." She led me to the couch where we both sat down. Jennifer lifted one of the big cookies to my lips. "Try it."

I bit into it and thought I'd gone to heaven. It was warm and chocolately and just the right chewy consistency. The perfect chocolate chip cookie. I moaned and finished it off.

"Mmm. Unbelievable . . . can I please have another?"

Mrs. McCoy was beaming. Obviously, the way to her heart was through flattery. "Of course, dear. Have as many as you wish."

For the next fifteen minutes, Jen and I feasted on the scrumptious melt-in-your-mouth cookies and hot chocolate while the McCoys recounted their afternoon with the Joneses. I flicked a crumb off Jennifer's lips— a small, endearing action that was not missed by her father. He winked at me.

When we had consumed everything, Mrs. McCoy cleared the table. "Blake, dear, I hope you'll be staying for dinner. I'm making something from the cookbook Jennifer bought me. Chicken fajitas."

Jen looked at me beseechingly. The truth: I didn't want to leave her, but I hadn't really thought much about the rest of my stay. I didn't think it was a good idea to spend the night here again and overextend it. Plus, staying at a hotel in town might prove to be very sexy. I could fuck Jennifer's brains out in a big king-sized bed without the worry of her parents invading our privacy. There was also the Jacuzzi tub. *Mhmm.*

"Stay, Blake," Jen begged. Lust danced in her green eyes.

"Okay," I conceded. I thanked Mrs. McCoy for her generosity, but told her I would be heading to The

Grove Hotel after dinner.

"Are you sure, Blake?" asked Mrs. McCoy. "We'd love to have you stay another night."

"Yeah. I have a reservation there." *Stick to the plan.*

Disappointment fell over Jen's face. The truth: I was going to miss her tonight as much as she was going to miss me. Maybe we could figure out a way to have a discreet quickie before I left. Or I could invite her to the hotel for an après dinner drink and then some.

As I stood up to head to my room and freshen up for dinner, my cell phone rang. I slid it out of my jeans pocket and looked at the screen. It was my Las Vegas affiliate manager, Vera Nichols. She was probably calling just to wish me Merry Christmas.

"Excuse me. I've got take this."

The call was not what I was expecting. I could feel the blood drain from my body as Vera's voice faded. *Jesus fucking Christ!*

"I'll get there as fast as I can," I said and ended the call.

"Blake, is everything okay?" asked Jennifer. Her eyes flickered with concern.

"I'm sorry, everyone. I can't stay. I've got to fly to Vegas to handle a crisis."

"What's going on?" Jen's rosebud lips curved into a frown.

"Nothing you need to know about." She looked hurt.

There was no way I was going to tell her Don Springer had beaten up SIN-TV producer Eddie Falcon to within an inch of his life. Springer. That fucking bastard who'd almost raped her.

Two hours later, I was on the six o'clock United flight heading to Vegas.

Chapter 9

Blake

The plane touched down at McCarran airport at nine thirty, a few minutes before our scheduled arrival time. I immediately found a cab and headed to Sunrise Hospital where Eddie had been taken. After dropping my bags and skis off with reception, I met Vera in the waiting room outside the intensive care unit. She leapt from her chair and gave me a hug.

"Oh, Blake. Thank you for coming."

"How's he doing?"

"He was badly beaten up. A couple of fractured ribs, a puncture to one of his lungs, and a concussion. He was in surgery for three hours to repair his lung."

Fuck. "Where did the attack take place?"

"Right outside his house. Springer followed him home."

There was only one more thing I desperately needed to know. "Did they catch him?"

"Not yet. There's a manhunt out for him."

"The fucker!" I growled. I wanted to find him myself and give him what he deserved.

Casually dressed in jeans and a Christmasy snow-man sweater, Vera looked weary. She should be home with her family celebrating Christmas. "Are you okay?" I asked.

She ran her hand through her short blond hair and blew out a sharp breath. "Yeah. But it's been a stressful day." She sat back down. I lowered myself onto the armchair next to hers and joined her.

"How's your family?"

"They're good. I'm just sorry I couldn't spend the rest of Christmas Day with them."

A dark thought crossed my mind. If Springer was on the loose, Vera and her family might be in danger. "Vera, I want you and your family to have around-the-clock police protection."

She held my gaze fierce in her toffee eyes. The thought had crossed her mind too. Springer was a sicko. There was no telling what he was capable of.

"The police aren't willing to do that. There's been no direct threat to me or my family." She chewed down on her lip. She was clearly worried.

"Forget the police. I'll set up private surveillance."

"But, Blake, that'll cost so much money. I can't afford that."

"Don't worry about the money. The company will pay for it. I need you, Vera." I couldn't bear to lose her and would be devastated if anything happened to her or her family.

Vera gave me another hug. "Thanks, Blake. I really appreciate it. You're the best."

A warm feeling warded off the chill of knowing Springer was out there. Somewhere. From the corner of my eye, I saw a doctor heading our way. He had a smattering of salt and pepper hair and wore rimless glasses.

"I'm Dr. Walters, the lead physician looking after Eddie Falcon."

"How's he doing?" I asked anxiously.

The doctor lifted his glasses on top of his balding head. I'd watched enough television shows to know that wasn't a good sign. My heart pounded with apprehension.

"He's a lucky man. He's going to be all right. We're going to keep him here a few days for observation."

I sighed with relief. So did Vera.

"Can we see him?" she asked.

The doctor nodded. "Yes. But he's very tired and on a morphine drip. So keep the visit short. He's in Room 520."

We thanked the doctor and together headed down the hall to Eddie's room.

Nothing prepared me for the sight of Eddie. Besides being hooked up to a bunch of beeping machines and tubes, his eyes were swollen shut, a wide bandage covered his head, and he was caked with dry blood from cuts and bruises everywhere. Bile rose to the back of my throat.

Vera and I sat down in a pair of armchairs close to his bed. He cracked a small smile upon seeing us.

"Hi, boss." His voice was a hoarse whisper. "Not such a merry Christmas."

I didn't know what to say. "You're going to be okay, Eddie."

"That's what the doc said. Did they catch the motherfucker?"

My heart sunk to my stomach. I wanted so much to tell him yes. I bowed my head and shook it. "Not yet, but they're going to. And when they do, I'm going to make sure that bastard burns in hell."

Rage coursed through my blood like an angry cobra. I was going to bring that motherfucker down whatever it took, even if I had to hunt him down myself.

Vera chimed in. "The doctor said you'll be going home in a few days."

Eddie was going to need police protection too.

Vera continued. "I called your ex-wife. She's going to fly in tomorrow from Miami and look after you."

A ray of happiness glinted in Eddie's swollen eyes. "She's a good girl. Wish it had worked out."

Eddie and his wife had recently divorced. She hated living in Vegas and even more so, couldn't take Eddie's porn career. Being in this business wasn't easy. I had to give credit to Vera and her husband for keeping it together.

Eddie's eyelids began to lower. It was a signal for us to leave. He needed rest.

I stood up. Vera followed suit.

"Take care, man. And trust me, we're going to nail that motherfucker."

Vera asked me if I wanted to grab a bite in the hospital's cafeteria. Having not eaten dinner and drained, I readily agreed.

Though cheerfully decorated for the holidays, there was something very depressing about having dinner here on Christmas Day. There were not many diners— just some weary looking doctors and nurses and a handful of glum-eyed visitors. Having a loved one who was sick in the hospital over Christmas must be very depressing. A pang of sadness hit me in the gut as I bit into my tuna fish sandwich. Vera had ordered the same along with two coffees.

She took a bite of the sandwich and put it down. "Blake, I meant to thank you for the generous bonus. I was blown away."

I smiled. On top of her six-figure salary, I'd given her a hefty $50,000 bonus. She was worth her weight in gold. "You deserved it. Our Vegas affiliate is our number one station thanks to you."

Her smile widened. "I love what I do. And I love working with you. Thanks to the bonus, we're finally going to be able to remodel our kitchen."

"That's great." I took a sip of my coffee.

"Oh, I also want to thank you for the boxful of *Power Ranger* toys you sent to Joshua. He went bananas. He's going to write you a thank-you note."

Joshua was her six-year-old son. Unlike my obnoxious twin nephews, he was a great kid. Polite and precocious. Despite her hectic, high-powered job, Vera had done a great job bringing him up. If I ever had a son, I hoped he'd be a lot like Josh. It would, of course, take a special woman to instill him with love and the right values. Jennifer's beautiful face flashed into my head. My heart hammered. Fuck. I missed her.

As if she were a mind reader, Vera asked, "How's it going with Jennifer?"

I could feel my face light up. "She broke up with her fiancé."

Vera high-fived me. "Congratulations."

"I followed your advice. Proved to her that Dickwick was not the right guy for her." I wasn't going to tell her how I did that. No way. That video I took of him and his hygienist was no one's business. I sure hoped she wasn't going to ask for details. Thank fucking God, she didn't.

"And so . . ."

My face heated up. Electricity coursed through my

blood vessels and I could feel my cock stir. "I told her I loved her."

"Oh my!" A cheek-to-cheek smile spread across her kind face.

I don't know what made me do it, but I launched into my story of surprising her at her house in Boise. And chatted away about the time we spent together.

"Blake Burns, you surprise me. You are quite the romantic."

I felt my face flush with embarrassment. Yup, the former Mr. Hook-Up was now a contender for the title, Mr. Romance. I inwardly had to laugh at myself.

We finished our sandwiches and drank the coffee to the last drop.

"Blake, where are you staying tonight?"

Fuck. I hadn't made any arrangements. Vegas hotels were probably booked up because of the holidays. I shrugged my shoulders. "I don't know. I don't have a hotel reservation."

She smiled warmly. "You don't need one. Stay at our place. We have a spare bedroom, and I'm sure Joshua will be thrilled to see you."

At first I hesitated, but then took her up on her kind offer. Besides, I wanted to be there in case fucking Springer showed up. Mental note: Make sure Vera has twenty-four hour surveillance.

Vera's house was a modest sixties contemporary located not far from the hospital. It was great to see her good-natured husband Steve with whom I shared a cigar and, of course, little Josh, who roped me into playing Power Rangers with him. I asked if he liked SpongeBob.

He rolled his eyes at me. "Uncle Blake, SpongeBob rules!"

I immediately thought again of my beautiful tiger.

After setting up security for Vera and her family as well as for Eddie, I called her. To my disappointment, her phone went straight to voice mail. I told her everything was okay in Vegas and that I would be heading back to LA in the morning. My last words: "I love you."

I went to bed in the small but comfortable guest room with my cell phone by my ear. I called Jen again and texted. *Nada.* I even tried calling her parents, but damn it, their phone number was unlisted. This Christmas Day, which had started out so great, had ended up with tragedy and uncertainty. Maybe I'd blown it with Jennifer leaving her so abruptly with little explanation. With a heavy heart, I finally succumbed to sleep.

I woke up in the morning to the smell of fresh coffee. Though the guest bed at Vera's house was as comfortable as could be, I slept like shit. All night long, I tossed and turned thinking about Jennifer, and having fucking Springer on my mind didn't help. Before getting out of bed, I stretched my arm to the nightstand where I'd moved my phone. I quickly checked my texts and messages. Not a word from my tiger despite how many times I'd tried to contact her. For sure, I'd fucked up again.

Feeling blue as balls, I staggered out of bed, did my usual morning routines in the adjacent guest bathroom, and then threw on some sweats. I could use a good hot cup of java. It wasn't even seven o'clock. Having an active six-year-old in the house did not make for sleeping in. I remembered those days well. I was a holy terror. My parents were lucky they could afford nannies to run after me.

Vera and her family were already at the breakfast table when I showed up. The kitchen was indeed a little run-down with old appliances and cabinets. I was glad Vera was going to be able to spruce it up with her bonus money.

"Hi, Uncle Blake," said Josh, playing with one of his Power Ranger action figures while eating his breakfast.

"Hi, Josh," I said with faux cheeriness.

Vera's husband Steve, dressed in pajamas, also welcomed me.

Vera, wearing a long white silky robe that looked brand new, was at the stove stirring a pot of what must be oatmeal. Hearing my voice, she turned around. I noticed her robe bore the insignia of Gloria's Secret—a small hot pink heart on the top pocket. Maybe it was a Christmas present from Steve.

"Good morning, Blake. What can I get you?"

"A cup of coffee would be great. And whatever you're making." Truthfully, I wasn't hungry. I took a seat at the table, and Vera brought me both a mug of coffee and a bowl of oatmeal. I took a sip of the hot beverage and instantly felt the caffeine rush into my bloodstream. I took another sip and my spirits lifted a teensy bit.

Just as Vera was about to join us at the table, the phone rang. She dashed over to a kitchen counter to pick it up. She listened intently and then broke into a smile.

"Thank you for letting me know," she said and hung up the phone.

Still wearing a smile and holding a mug of coffee, she sat down at the table facing me. She was extremely pretty. She wore her blond hair short, and a combination of warmth and intelligence radiated from her toffee brown eyes. She was so different from the blond bimboes I dated. I mean, *used* to date.

"Great news, Blake. They caught Don Springer."

My eyes lit up. "Where'd they find him?"

She took a sip of her coffee. "The police picked him up at the airport."

"Thank f—God." I managed not to say the f-word in front of Josh. Springer was lucky. Man, if I had found him, I would have cut off his balls and maybe cut out his heart. I could never forgive him for what he did to Jennifer. Or to poor Eddie.

Vera's husband Steve was also relieved.

"Who's Don *Spwinger?*" asked Josh, who had an adorable speech impediment because he was missing a front tooth.

Vera ruffled her fingers through his sandy hair. "No one you know, mister. Now get going. Daddy's going to take you bike riding this morning."

Finishing his milk, Josh jumped up. "Come on, Daddy. Hurry. Let's go," he shouted as he scooted out of the room.

Steve rose from the table. "Gotta go. Will I be seeing you later, Blake?"

"Not sure. Probably not."

"Well good to see you, man, and thanks for the cigar." He winked at me. "Don't mess with my wife."

Steve knew about my reputation as a player, but he had a sense of humor about it. Moreover, his marriage was rock solid, and he knew I loved and respected Vera. She was more than a fellow employee. She was a dear friend and almost like a sister to me.

"Don't worry," I said with a little laugh. He gave Vera peck on the cheek and followed his son out the door.

Vera sipped her coffee. "I'm glad that's over."

"Me too. Springer's going to be doing a good amount of time." *Life behind bars would be better*, I silently added. *The fucking animal.*

Vera smiled. "Well, I guess you can go back to Boise and spend the rest of your holiday with Jennifer."

I twisted my mouth. "Can't. Jennifer doesn't want to see me."

Vera's knitted her brows. "What do you mean?"

"She hasn't answered any of my texts or calls."

"What's going on?"

"She probably thinks I came to Vegas to see some babe. I didn't tell her the real reason for splitting."

Vera rolled her eyes. "Jesus, Blake. Why didn't you tell her?"

"I was afraid to. She was with her parents. I didn't want to upset them or her."

"Well, Blake, she's a big girl and could have handled it. Call her again and tell her the truth. If you don't, I will."

"It's futile. She's not going to pick up her phone. She's stubborn that way."

"Well then, call her house."

"The number's not listed."

"Blake, I'm sure you can get it from Mrs. Cho or your Human Resources person. It must be listed on some form she filled out asking for emergency contacts."

I twitched a smile. Vera was right. Why didn't I think of that?

Where's there's a will, there's a way. I pulled out my cell phone from a pocket of my sweats and immediately speed-dialed Mrs. Cho's home number. My super-organized secretary would for sure have it in some file. A glimmer of hope slithered through me.

I nervously drummed the table with my fingers while waiting for Mrs. Cho to pick up. She did on the second ring. Two minutes later, I had all the phone numbers associated with Jennifer's parents. Both their home number and their cell phones. Spotting a loose crayon on the table, I scribbled them down a paper napkin. God bless, Mrs. Cho.

"Bingo," I shouted as I dialed Harold McCoy's cell phone. I didn't want to run the risk of Jen picking up the home phone and hanging up on me.

As I anxiously waited for him to pick up, my eyes stayed riveted on smiling Vera. Her robe had given me another idea.

If things worked out with Jennifer—man, they'd better—I was going to call Gloria and Jaime up next and ask them for a favor. Things were looking up.

Chapter 10

Jennifer

I'd cried myself to sleep. When I woke up in the morning, I felt worse than last night. Blake Burns had ripped my heart apart. He had told me loved me, given me the best twenty-four hours of my life, and then left me bereft. Yeah, some big emergency in Vegas. Maybe one of his bimbos was having a break-down from Blake withdrawal or her breast implants were leaking. Or a Vegas orgy. Calling Blake Burns.

A sadness like I'd never known consumed every cell of my body. Why couldn't I feel numb or angry? At least, if I were angry, I could make some decisions. I'd never felt this way when I broke up with Bradley whom I'd known for over five years. I hadn't even known Blake for five weeks and the ache in my heart was unbearable. My eyes stung and my throat constricted. I could barely breathe.

Slowly, I rolled out of bed and took small, unsteady steps to the bathroom. I could hardly walk. I caught a glimpse of myself in the mirror. I looked worse than I thought. My eyes were red and puffy, my lips swollen,

.

and my skin blotchy. I watched as another round of tears trickled down my face.

Somehow I managed to get downstairs. My early-riser parents were already seated at the kitchen table. They stared at me. Given what I looked like, I expected my mother to grow panicky and run up to me and give me a big hug. She didn't.

"Jan Lunden called me late last night. She took her granddaughter to a movie yesterday and told me she saw you there."

Jan was an old friend of my mother's. A bridge pal. I froze.

"She said she saw you with your fiancé. Kissing him."

Silence. The only thing that roared in my ear was my hammering heart.

"I asked her what he looked like."

My heart beat faster.

"She described someone that sounds exactly like Blake."

I could no longer hold back. I burst into sobs. A torrent of tears stormed down my face.

My father spoke softly as I stood there heaving, bawling uncontrollably. "Jennie, come here and tell your mother what's going on."

I staggered to the table and collapsed into a chair. "Mom, I fell in love with Blake Burns and last night he broke my heart."

My mother was wide-eyed with shock. My father looked at me compassionately.

"Now, honey, tell your mother who Blake is."

"My b-boss," I stammered through my tears. I didn't tell her he was the head of a porn channel. I glanced at my father. Did he know? His knowing eyes told me did. *Please, Dad, don't say anything. Please!* I just didn't need to make matters worse. My mother would have a stroke if she knew.

To my relief, he said nothing as my mother jumped up. She gabbed a linen napkin and came around the table.

"Darling, why didn't you tell us?" She gave me a much-needed hug and dabbed my tears.

"I don't know. It's complicated, and it all happened so fast."

The tears kept falling. I took the napkin from my mother and brushed them away.

"But, darling, I don't understand. Why do you think he's hurt you?"

"Mom, he's a player."

A puzzled expression swept over her face. She didn't know what that meant.

"He dates lots of girls. I'm just one of them. He went to Vegas last night to see someone else. "

Mom furrowed her brows. "What makes you think that? He seemed so serious when he took that call. He said there was a crisis."

My father responded. "I agree with your mother. I trust Blake."

How could he trust him after only knowing him for twenty-four hours? I loved and respected my father, but he didn't know my boss the way I did. My father continued.

"He gave me his word he wouldn't hurt you. Jennie baby, I believe him."

Before I could say another word, a phone rang. I recognized the ringtone. My father's. John Lennon's "Love," my parents' wedding song.

Retrieving it from the kitchen counter where it was plugged in and recharging, he spoke into it as he headed back to the table.

"Yes, Blake, she's right here. I'll put you on with her."

How the hell did Blake get his number? My heart-beat went into a frenzy. I was practically hyperventilat-ing. My dad sat back down at the table and told Blake to "hold on."

"Dad, I don't want to speak to him."

"I'm your father. Please hear him out." He handed me the phone.

I took a deep breath to fortify myself and swiped away my tears with my free hand. Trembling, I put the phone to my ear.

"Hello." My voice was small and shaky.

His voice was loud and strong. The sound of it

rattled me. He told me he wanted me to take the call away from my parents. He had something to tell me.

"Okay." I breathed out the word, and rising, told my parents I'd be right back. I moved into the living room and slumped onto the couch. I let Blake know I was alone.

Blake: "Jennifer, you need to know the real reason I went to Vegas."

Me: "And what might that be?" My quivering voice was dripping with sarcasm.

Blake: "Don Springer."

The mention of his name stunned me into silence.

Blake: "Jen, are you there? Can you hear me?"

Me: "Yes." My voice was just above whisper.

Blake: "He beat up the producer of *Private Dick*."

I gasped and every muscle in my body tensed. I knew Blake couldn't be lying. Not about something like that. Guilt stabbed at my heart. I should have trusted him.

Me: "Oh my God. Is he okay?"

Blake: "Yes, and they've got the motherfucker in custody."

A new round of tears assaulted me. Tears of relief and remorse.

Me: "Oh, Blake. I'm so sorry."

Blake: "Sorry about what, tiger?"

Me: "That I mistrusted you."

Blake: "You had the right to. I fucked up. I should

have told you the truth. I was afraid."

Me: "I understand." My man wanted to protect me, shelter me from the monsters of the world.

Blake: "Baby, I love you."

Me: "I love you too." Oh God, did I love him!

Blake: "When are you heading back to LA?"

Me: "The thirty-first."

Blake: "I have some Springer shit I have to deal with in Vegas and then I'm heading back. I want to spend New Years with you.

A new year. A new beginning.

Me: "Okay." A squeak.

Blake: "Send me your flight info. I'll pick you up."

Me: "I will."

Blake: "Tiger, just know. I love you. There's no one but you."

I fingered the gemstone heart around my neck and glanced at the snow tiger I'd left on the couch. With my free arm, I reached for him and hugged him tight against me.

Me: "Blake, I love you too."

We ended the call, and I found myself crying more buckets of tears. Except they were tears of joy. There were no Scrabble words to describe how much I loved Blake Burns.

Chapter 11

Jennifer

The next five days at home were happy ones. I told my parents things were again great between Blake and me. That there had just been a misunderstanding. There was no way I was going to tell them about Don Springer. They'd freak. The past was the past. He was going to jail, and I was going to put him out of mind.

Both my parents, however, were concerned about how I was going to handle my relationship at work. I told them Blake and I were going to figure things out. I also told them Blake's father was the head of Conquest Broadcasting. Dad already knew that. I was positive my inquisitive dad had googled Blake and knew he headed up SIN-TV. I was grateful he didn't tell my mother while I was home. Though at some point, she was going to have to find out.

Although I enjoyed spending time with Mom and Dad, I counted the days, the hours, and the minutes until going back to LA and seeing Blake. He called and texted me all day long. We even Skyped. When I saw his gorgeousness on my computer screen, I wanted to jump through it and be in his arms. I lost count of how many times we exchanged the words "I love you." I couldn't say or hear them enough.

Finally, the thirty-first rolled around. Bradley had cut my time with my parents short because he had planned to take me to a New Year's Eve party given by one of his boring dentist friends. I actually looked into getting a flight home sooner—I so badly wanted to be with Blake—but the cheapskate had booked a non-refundable ticket that you couldn't change. On top if it, there were no flights available.

My flight was in the morning. I was grateful there wasn't another snowstorm. After hugging my mother good-bye and collecting a bagful of cookies she'd baked for me to take back, my dad drove me to the airport. His favorite classical music station played while I held Blake's plush tiger on my lap and stared out the window dreaming about him. Dad's soothing voice cut into my reverie.

"Jennie, what are you doing for New Year's Eve?"

"I'm spending it with Blake, but I don't know what we're doing."

He nodded. "He's a good man. I like him a lot."

Somehow, I felt like this was the moment to ask him. "Dad, do you know exactly what he does?"

"He heads the porn channel you work at."

Though his voice was nonchalant and nonjudgmental, my skin bristled.

"How do you feel about that?" I asked nervously.

"My Jennie, you're a big girl now. You have to make your own decisions."

"Dad, I really love what I do and I'm good at it."

A small smile played on his handsome profile. "I know. And I'm proud of you, Jennie McCoy."

I was beaming. "Thanks, Dad." I paused. "Are you going to tell Mom?"

"Yep."

I swallowed hard. "How do you think she'll react?"

"You'll hear her shrieking from Los Angeles, but she'll get over it."

I laughed with relief. I so loved my dad.

In no time, we arrived at the airport. At the curb, I put the tiger into the large shopping bag with the cookies and hugged my dad good-bye. About to enter the terminal, I turned to wave at him. "I love you, Dad," I shouted out. He blew me a kiss I caught with my heart. The next kiss was going to be Blake's. My heart raced. I couldn't wait.

Exactly two hours and ten minutes later, he was there. Waiting for me in the LAX terminal at arrivals. It was impossible to miss him. Besides being the most devastating man in the crowd, he was holding a monstrous SpongeBob balloon that said, "Soak it up!"

I soaked him up. My heart almost beat out of my chest. Dressed casually in jeans and a tee, he wore a cheek-to-cheek smile on his ravishing face and looked hotter than hell. I dropped my bags and ran into his arms. He crushed his delicious lips on mine and spun me around and around. I was still wearing my winter coat and wooly hat.

"Oh, Blake! I've missed you so much."

"Me too, baby. C'mon, let's get out of here."

Within ten minutes of being in Blake's Porsche, I realized he wasn't taking me home. We were on the 10 Freeway heading toward Santa Monica. The whole country was experiencing frigid conditions, but here in LA the weather was unseasonably summer-like. The top was down. I'd shed my coat and hat, and my hair blew in the warm wind.

"Where are we going?" I shouted above the loud whooshing sound.

"The balloon is a clue."

I gazed up at the silly balloon. He'd tied the long string around a side mirror, and it was whipping around in the air. SpongeBob lived in the ocean. So, maybe he was taking me for lunch at Back on the Beach, the restaurant where we'd shared our first meal together after our unforgettable Santa Monica Steps workout.

The memory of that day flashed into my head. How he'd carried me up all those steps when I'd gotten a cramp and then massaged my leg to the point of arousal. Tingling all over, I smiled as the 10 turned into the Pacific Coast Highway and the ocean magically appeared.

Being from the landlocked Midwest, the view of the white-crested Pacific Ocean on one side and the flower-covered craggy hills on the other, never ceased to amaze me. Today the water was a rare aquamarine, the waves majestic. There was only one view more breathtaking—that of the man sitting next to me with one hand on the wheel, the other on my thigh. As the wind ruffled his dark silky hair, I absorbed the invigorating salty scent of the ocean air. The Lumineers were playing on the radio. Between the gusting wind and blasting music, it was difficult to talk and be heard. But I was fine with the silence. Intermittently, a smile slid on Blake's beautiful face and I wondered what he was thinking. Hopefully, the same thing I was: I belong to you; you belong to me.

To my surprise, we passed by Back on the Beach. We didn't stop. Blake had another destination in mind.

"Okay, Mr. Burns, tell me where we're going."

He tugged at my flapping ponytail and smiled wryly. "It's a surprise."

The throbbing between my legs intensified and my heartbeat quickened. Blake was all about surprises. And usually a surprise came with one thing. His spectacular cock. My breathing hitched.

About forty minutes into the ride, the scenery along the PCH became significantly more rugged. The beach houses lining the narrow highway disappeared, replaced by towering cypress trees that obscured the ocean view. I begged Blake again to tell me where he was taking me.

Blake stole a look at me and smiled his heartstopping dimpled smile. "You'll see in a few minutes."

Sure enough, five minutes later, the car turned left onto an almost hidden road. Blake slowed down as he expertly navigated a rocky serpentine path. On either side of the rustic road, tall trees mixed with wild grass and flowers. The scent of the foliage mingled with that of the sea and was divine enough to bottle. A staggering all-glass structure came into view. Blake pulled into the impressive pebbled driveway. Semi-circular in shape, it could easily accommodate a dozen vehicles.

I gawked at the architecturally magnificent edifice. It was something straight out of one of those expensive interior design magazines with its multi-level planes and angles. And it was huge. Like a mini museum or something. Most amazing of all, it sat on a cliff and overlooked the ocean.

"We've reached our final destination," Blake said as he hopped out of the car and came around to open my door. I stepped out of the Porsche.

My round-as-marbles eyes drank in my surroundings. "What is this place?"

"It's Jaime Zander's beach house. He and Gloria are away with the twins and offered to let me use it."

"Oh my God, it's fabulous," I exclaimed as Blake took hold of my hand and led me to the entrance. I remembered Jaime mentioning he and his family were heading to Hawaii over the holidays when we'd had lunch together.

Inside, the house was even more fabulous than I could imagine. A contemporary glass palace with floor-to-ceiling windows, offering glorious views of the Pacific. The furnishings were modern, sparse, and oversized, mostly in shades of white. The all-white interior showed off the colorful abstract paintings that lined the walls, all signed PAZ—an acronym for Payton Anthony Zander, Jaime's late father. The artist who had painted *The Kiss*, the masterpiece Blake had given me. Framed photos were scattered everywhere, from the white lacquered baby grand to the immense fireplace mantle, and added warmth to the interior. I ambled over to the piano and studied the photos. In the center was a large one of a stunning couple embracing on the beach on their wedding day—Jaime and Gloria. Surrounding this centerpiece, were other photos of the couple along with numerous photos of their adorable twins—Payton and Paulette.

"They look like the perfect family."

"They are," beamed Jaime. "Wait here for a minute. I'm going to get our bags."

Wait! We're staying here? Before I could ask, Blake was out the door. He was back in a flash with my rollerbag, his overnight case, and the bagful of my mom's cookies. And my tiger.

"Come on, let's go to the guest room and unload our stuff."

I got a chance to ask my question. "Are we staying here?"

He smacked my lips with a kiss. "All weekend. Do you have a problem with that?"

"But Blake, I hardly have a thing to wear. Almost everything in my suitcase is for cold weather."

"Don't worry about it." Smirking, he scanned my body. "You won't be needing much."

My heart skipped a beat and a tingle shot up my middle. For sure, Blake had the weekend well planned with one activity in mind. Fine by me.

Taking our bags, my gorgeous sex god led me up a baby-proofed winding stairs that evoked the curl of a wave. There were numerous rooms on the second level, including an adorable nursery. The guest room meant to be ours was at the very end of a long hallway. It, too, was all white. Anchoring it—an inviting bleached wood king-sized bed covered with a plush duvet and a mountain of fluffy pillows. Blake plopped our stuff onto a nearby luggage rack while I gravitated to a huge hot pink box on the bed. The size of a suitcase, it was meticulously wrapped with a white bow as big as a basketball. I eyed a small envelope tucked inside the ribbon with my name beautifully written on it.

"What's this?" I asked Blake.

"A present from Gloria."

"You're kidding!" Gloria's Secret was the largest lingerie retailer in the world, though I'd never bought much there except my cherry vanilla shampoo. Right after the holidays, I was pitching her my concept for a SIN-TV daytime block targeted at women. The PowerPoint presentation was close to being finished.

"Open it," Blake insisted.

Eagerly, I reached for the envelope first. Inside was a note handwritten in the same elegant scroll.

Dear Jennifer~

Enjoy! Hope you have a wonderful weekend! Look forward to meeting you soon!

xo~Gloria

I placed the note on the bed beside the box and proceeded to open it. Upon removing the lid, my eyes grew wide. Beneath layers of delicate pink tissue paper was a barrage of beautifully folded lingerie. Dozens of matching silk bras and bikinis in different colors and patterns, baby dolls, plus a magnificent robe. Each piece exquisite. As I dug further, I discovered the package also included Gloria's Secret outerwear—floral sundresses, shorts and tops, sweats as well as a couple of sexy bikinis and a pair of flip-flops. Even a sparkly black mini dress and matching stilettos. Everything I needed for a New Year's weekend at the beach and all in my size.

"Oh my God!" I was overwhelmed. "I can't accept all this."

Blake wrapped his arms around me from behind, and I could feel his warm breath tickle the nape of my neck. "Get over it. Gloria will be insulted. And besides, it's all really a gift for me."

A delicious shiver skittered down my spine as he began to unbutton my blouse and lower it past my shoulders. His hands skimmed my breasts, and I could feel my nipples peaking. Wetness was already pooling between my legs as the blouse fell to the floor.

"Get undressed," Blake whispered in my ear. As he nuzzled my neck, heating every bit of me, I managed to undo the zipper of my jeans and step out of them after kicking off my shoes. My breathing grew uneven as he unhooked my bra and slid it down my arms while I stepped out of my panties.

"I want you to give me a fashion show." He reached for a random matching bra and thong. Turquoise lace with pearl embellishments. "Put these on first," he ordered, handing them to me. He rifled through the box. "And put the stilettos on too."

I slipped on the lingerie, then the shoes, and stood before him. I was as stiff as a board. His lustful eyes roamed my body.

"C'mon, baby. Loosen up." Hopping into the bed, he hit a remote and Beyoncé filled the room.

I loved Beyoncé. She had a great voice and was all about woman-power. As she sang "Crazy in Love," I paraded around the bed as gracefully as I could.

Blake leaned against the headboard, his arms folded across his broad chest and his long muscular legs outstretched. His smoldering eyes followed me, and a contented smile splayed across his face.

"Next," he said, his voice sultry.

I quickly stripped off the lingerie I was wearing and put on another set—a red lace strapless bra and matching thong. Blake gave me a thumbs up.

The music got to me. He got to me. I found myself doing things I'd never done before. Pushing up my boobs. Swaying my hips. Sliding my hand beneath the lace. Throwing my ass into his face. Pouting and blowing him kisses. Even singing along. I was enjoying every moment. And so was he. I'd never felt so sexy.

On my third change of lingerie—a sheer polka dot baby doll—he signaled me to come over to him with a curl of his finger.

Heated, I crawled onto the bed and faced him on my hands and knees. My roaring tiger pose. To my astonishment, I actually let out a fierce growl.

"Come here, my sexy little supermodel," he rasped. His eyes were hooded.

I scooted up closer to him. He unzipped his fly. Out popped his monstrous cock. There was already a bead of pre-cum on the tip. My breathing hitched.

"Have you missed this, tiger?"

I clutched my galloping heart like I was having an attack and breathed out, "Yes."

"As much as I've missed this?" Without warning, he tore off the scrap of fabric I was wearing and plunged a long finger deep into my pussy. I gasped.

And gasped again when he put his finger, glistening with my juices, to his mouth and sucked it.

"Mmmm. I might eat you for dinner, but right now, I want you to sit on my cock. And ride me."

Despite how loosened up I was, my body trembled. I'd never done this position before. What I knew from books I read, it was incredible. Deep and empowering. I repositioned myself so I was straddling his hips. Slowly, I lowered myself onto his huge erection. Upon entry, I yelped with pleasure. I was so wet his extraordinary length seated me in no time.

"Oh, Blake! You feel so good," I moaned out. God, he felt divine. So hot! So big! So mine!

"You *really* have missed me, baby." He lifted the sheer baby doll top and groped my breasts. As he kneaded them, his thumbs circled around my tender nipples, sending a rush of erotic sensations to my core. I bit down on my lip. The combination of his fullness and my flutters was already sending me over the edge.

Drunk with lust, his eyes fixed on mine. "Now, tiger, anchor your hands on the bed, lift your hips, and come down on me again. Hard."

I did as bid and quickly got into a rhythm. While I could feel him thrusting into me, he let me control the pace and depth of penetration. I rode him hard and fast, working myself into a sweat. Every time I had sex with Blake, I thought it couldn't get better. But this was amazing. Fucking amazing! Each time I ground down on him, he bucked into me, stimulating my clit and hitting my magic spot again and again. *Oh! Oh! Oh! Oh!* My greedy mouth sucked every ounce of flesh it could reach and chewed on his damp tee.

The beginnings of a major orgasm descended on me quickly. I was leaving this earth. Falling off a cliff. My fingernails clawed the crisp cotton sheet. I was sure it was torn.

"Blake, I'm going to come," I cried out.

"Keep your eyes open, and I want to hear you roar my name until you're hoarse."

With whimpering pants that bordered on sobs, I nodded. As he continued to pummel into me, my climax spiraled, consuming every cell in its path like a fierce tornado. I roared his name until my throat was sore.

"Fuck, tiger!" he shouted as his own orgasm collided with mine. His body jerked as he spurted his hot semen inside me. Our eyes never broke contact.

"Fuck," he said again with a harsh breath as he pumped one more blast into my quivering pussy.

A heated sheen coated his face and I could practically see my reflection. He leaned forward to reward me with a kiss. I cupped his strong jaw in my hands to prolong it. His mouth was delicious, his tongue so talented. I never wanted his kisses to end.

Recovering from my powerful orgasm, I finally pulled away. His cock was still in me. Leaning his head back against the headboard, he gazed at me and traced my face softly with his hand.

"Tiger, do you know why you're so sexy and beautiful?"

I shook my head. No man had ever used those words to describe me.

A smile played on his face. "Because you don't know it."

I smiled back at him. "I do know something."

"And what might that be?" he asked slyly.

"That I love you."

In a breath, he rolled me over and was pummeling me again.

His heart was in his eyes when he repeated my words and breathed out one word with one final powerful thrust: "Mine."

We came together.

We spent the rest of the afternoon fucking and cuddling. We shared silly intimate things like childhood stories, dreams, and scars. While I had many, each with a story that captivated him, Mr. Beautiful only had one small battle scar on his back—the result of a fight he'd had with his sister, Marcy, when he was a youngster. The stories he told me about the two of them growing up together had me roaring with laughter. The funniest of all was the time his sister, ten years older and a gynecologist, found him in her office fucking one of his high school teachers with her feet in the stirrups. I laughed until I cried. Blake Burns was indeed a very naughty boy and I loved him all the more for it.

Outside, the sound of waves crashing against the rocky shoreline sounded in my ears. Before long, the sky darkened, and exhausted from all the love and laughter, I dozed off, tucked in his brawny arm with my head on his warm taut chest. His heart beat like a lullaby in my ears.

When we awoke, it was almost eight o'clock. Ravenous after a long, mind-blowing shower, we dressed casually in sweats and made dinner together in the enormous, state-of-the-art kitchen. The menu: lobster, champagne, and my mother's chocolate chip cookies. He'd bought the lobsters and champagne before picking me up at the airport.

I'd never eaten lobster before, and I had a hard time dropping the live, red-shelled creature into a large pot of warm water that was going to put it to sleep before it boiled away. Blake had told me this was a less cruel way of preparing the delicacy—the lobster would feel no pain—but it didn't really help.

"Blake, I can't do it!" I cried, holding the monstrous squirming crustacean in my hand. I was practically in tears.

"Think about some one you hate and name the lobster after him. It helps." Standing behind me, he pressed his erection into my backside and blew hotly on my neck. "I named mine Springer."

I visibly shuddered. Though Springer was now behind bars, the mention of him triggered a shiver that zigzagged down my spine. The claws of my lobster snapped, adding further to my distress.

Blake noticed my unease and tenderly kissed the top of my head. "I'm sorry, baby. I shouldn't have said his name." He glanced at my agitated lobster. "Do you want me to put your lobster in the pot?"

"No, I want to do it," I said, recovering and happy *that* monster was going to boil to death slowly.

Smiling, Blake asked me again, "So what's your guy's name?"

I stared at my big, red-clawed shellfish. A name instantly came to my mind. "Bradley." Yeah, my lobster looked like a Bradley. *Dickwick.* Laughing with me, Blake held me in his arms as I dropped Bradley into the pot and said adieu.

The lobsters took no time to cook, and we sat down to eat right at the island counter in the kitchen. Blake tied a silly lobster bib around my neck and showed me how to eat one with the help of a nutcracker and special pick-like fork. The irony of it all was that Bradley tasted so melt-in-your-mouth good with all that melted butter. Blake told me lobster was an aphrodisiac and an ideal source of low-fat protein, much needed for a long night of seduction. I believed him. I watched him expertly crack a claw, and as the snowy white meat poured out, I felt myself heated up and aroused. I took a sip of my bubbly champagne.

At a little before nine, Blake popped another bottle of champagne. He led me to a room off the kitchen and turned on one of the many TVs. Ryan Seacrest was hosting the ball drop at New York's Times Square where it was going on midnight. On a plush, comfy sofa, I curled up in Blake's arms and watched the crowd go wild with the countdown. *Five . . . four . . . three . . . two . . . one!*

As the ball crashed onto Times Square, Blake's lips crashed onto mine. The kiss was lush and lingering. *Auld Lang Syne* filtered in my ear. The original words of the poem.

Should Old Acquaintance be forgot, and never
thought upon;
The flames of Love extinguished, and fully past
and gone.

Bradley Wick, DDS, was now past, gone, and out of my life. There was only one man in the world for me who oddly shared a last name with Robert Burns, my father's favorite poet, who'd written these words. Blake Burns. His being consumed me and brought passionate tears to my eyes.

"Happy New Year, tiger," he said softly, gwawing at my lips.

"Happy New Year, Blake," I repeated, not able to get enough of him.

He made me insatiable and I did the same for him. We craved each other. Placing my hand on his heavy arousal, he breathed, "Let's end this year with a bang."

Blake, always full of surprises, had one more in store for me before the New Year dawned. The Jacuzzi. Big enough to accommodate a dozen people, it was built into an expansive deck outside the house.

Our bare bodies buried in the bubbly water, Blake sat close to me. One strapping arm curled around my shoulders while the hand of the other held a lit cigar.

The stars and the full moon sparkled overhead in the blackened sky. The steamy water gurgled while Céline Dion piped through hidden speakers, and in the near distance, I could hear the waves of the ocean softly ebb and flow. The intense warm jets of water sprayed my upper back and between my thighs, feeling so tingly good. I was in love, lust, and paradise. It couldn't get more magical than this.

"Tiger, do you mind if I smoke this cigar?" Blake asked, already blowing out a puff of smoke. "It's kind of a New Year's tradition."

I inhaled. The smell of the tobacco mixing with the salty sea air was heady. To my surprise, I loved it. I took the cigar from him and put it to my mouth. I inhaled and choked.

"No problem," I coughed out, reaching for my flute of champagne. I took a calming sip.

"Stop showing off," he laughed, taking the cigar back in his hand. He inhaled another puff and I glared at him. Mesmerized by the way he held the cigar between his long fingers and sucked on the tip, drawing in his cheeks and lowering his eyes. Equally sexy was the way he pursed his kissable lips and blew out the smoke.

"You know, baby. My father once told me a fine cigar is like a fine woman. You have to warm her before you assault her."

His words made my heart flutter. "Blake, when was

the first time you knew you loved me?" I asked as a ring of smoke mingled with the steam from the Jacuzzi.

He placed the cigar on a close by ashtray and turned to face me. His eyes glinted in the moonlight. Damn he was beautiful. And oh so sexy. He twirled my damp ponytail with his hand.

"It could have been love at first sight. When you kissed me blindfolded at my club. Something changed in me. Then after the Springer thing, I knew if something happened to you, I couldn't live. You're my air, baby. I need you to breathe."

A trail of sparks blazed through my body. He loved me right from the beginning. He repeated my question.

Tracing his kissable lips, I said, "Vegas. When I danced with you." Ironically, a Céline Dion version of "The First Time Ever I Saw Your Face," the song we danced to, was piping through the hidden speakers. Maybe he'd intentionally programmed it. I shifted a little and the powerful jet beneath me stimulated my clit.

He tugged at my ponytail. "It took you that long?" His voice was playfully miffed.

I twisted a smile. No, it hadn't. The truth: I think I'd loved him the minute my mouth set down on his in that game of Truth or Dare too. I'd felt the earth move in my heart. Maybe it was lust. It didn't matter because I wasn't going to tell him.

We imbibed some champagne and glanced up at the

starry sky. My head rested on his rugged chest.

"Jennifer, do you know why the moon and the stars shine?"

I shook my head. The words of the beautiful song were affecting me. The jets were affecting me. He was affecting me. Desire was bubbling inside me. "Why?"

Because they're making love to the sky."

"Lighting it up," I replied dreamily, my eyes focused on the many constellations above us.

He drew me closer. Passion sparked in his eyes. "Jennifer McCoy, you are my moon and shining star. My universe."

In a breath, I was sitting on top of him. Riding him to the heavens. Lighting him up. Lighting myself up.

We came together like comets flaring and whispered, in unison, three celestial words.

"I love you."

Chapter 12

Jennifer

I woke up to the sound of crashing waves and squawking gulls. Blinking my eyes open, I was still nestled in naked bliss against Blake's warm chest. One arm was wrapped around me, the other draped across the duvet. I swiveled my head and gazed at him. God, he was beautiful. His lush lips were parted slightly and strands of his bedhead hair fell forward onto his forehead. The morning sunlight beamed through the bedroom's wraparound windows and cast him in a golden haze. I couldn't help tracing my finger around his lightly stubbled jaw. He stirred and then his long-lashed eyelids flittered. Opening one eye at a time, he met my gaze.

"Hi." His raspy morning voice was sexy as sin as was the adorable lopsided smile that accompanied it.

"Hi," I echoed. I sounded like a shy kindergartener meeting her teacher on the first day of school. I just couldn't believe all this was real. That this was happening to me.

Keeping his half-closed, contemplative eyes trained

on me, he circled my lips with his index finger. The ticklish sensation sent a jolt of tingles to my already heated center. On the second rotation, my lips clamped down on his deft finger and sucked it. A sound, something between a hum and a moan, filled the back of my throat.

"Oh, baby," he moaned back. "You're fucking turning me on."

Expecting him to fuck me on the spot, he bolted up to a sitting position, taking me with him. He massaged my shoulders and breathed against my neck. "C'mon. Let's take a shower together."

With a smack of his lips against mine, he rolled off the bed and rose to his feet. My eyes traveled down his swoon-worthy body, with its chiseled six pack and perfect pelvic V that led to his rippled thighs and outrageous thick length. My gaze stayed glued on the latter. To say he was endowed was an understatement.

"What are you staring at?" That cocky smile flashed on his ravishing face.

"You." I felt my cheeks flush with embarrassment and impulsively flung the covers over my head.

With a swoosh, the covers came off. He was hovering above me. All six foot three of his manly gorgeousness.

"You can stare at me all you want in the shower. Now, come on."

Before I could say a word, I was in his arms, being

carried away to our first New Year's Day activity.

The guest bathroom was amazing. I'd never seen one like it except in those high-priced design magazines I peeked at while waiting in the supermarket checkout line. It was seriously bigger than my living room—all creamy tranquil marble with travertine floors and state-of-the-art fixtures. There was even a chaise lounge and a fireplace. A huge freestanding porcelain tub stood before a window overlooking the ocean, and by another, stood a glass-encased shower stall, the size of my bedroom. In fact, bigger.

Blake opened the shower door and set me down. He turned on several faucets and powerful jets of water sprayed me from everywhere. Blake drew me against him, my back to his chest. I could feel his erection against me.

"Are you going to fuck me?" I asked as he soaped me up and nuzzled my shoulders.

"Not until I do this first, tiger."

The soap fell out of his hand onto the slick marble floor, and I suddenly felt a slippery fingertip at my backdoor. I let out a yelp.

"Have you ever been touched here?" he asked.

"No," I gasped. Seriously, did he even have to ask?

"I want you to relax. It's just my finger. We'll take it slow and easy. And I'm going to make it so you love it." He kissed the nape of my neck and then purred. "This is all about you."

I tensed as he slowly slid his finger up my passage. A groan escaped my throat. And my flesh trembled.

"Does it hurt?"

"Just a little." Honestly, it was a weird, good kind of hurt. I just wasn't used to it.

"That's normal. You're so fucking tight. Don't worry, tiger. I'm going to loosen you up."

He slid his finger, lubricated from the soap, back down. As he gently pushed it back up, a finger of his other hand descended on my clit. He began to vigorously rub it.

"Oh, Blake!" I moaned, arching my body.

"Does that help?"

"Oh, yes." It was true. The divine pleasure between my thighs was allowing me to loosen up and enjoy what was going on behind.

"That's what I thought. A new year. A new sensation."

In my mind's eye, I could see the sexy smirk on his face. To be truthful, I'd never experienced a sensation like this. Though I'd had the little vibrating egg up my butt, this was different. I squeezed my eyes shut and let myself soak in the intensity of the pleasure. I was getting used to his finger in my butt. The unfamiliar yet fulfilling fullness. He continued to butt finger me and rub my clit for several minutes. I could still feel his hard length pressing against me. Little whimpers spilled from my mouth.

"Okay, baby, now we're going to take it up a notch." I bucked against him as he removed his deft finger from my clit and plunged it into my pussy.

"Oh my God!" I shrieked. He was pussy fingering me and butt fingering in tandem. The pressure was insane, especially when his fingers almost met. I was falling apart at the seams. My orgasm crescendoed. I couldn't hold back. My body trembled against his as I screamed my release. I felt like I'd broken into a million beautiful pieces.

Removing his fingers, Blake held me steady and nibbled my neck. "My father always says it's better to give than receive. Now, baby, I'm going to fuck you like there's no tomorrow."

It was the most outrageous shower I'd ever taken. Each time Blake fucked me, he brought me to a place I'd never been before. Making me feel glorious sensations that were new to me and titillating. I never knew before what my body was capable of. We'd ended the year with a bang, and now we'd started the new one with an even bigger one.

Buzzing all over, I wrapped myself in the thick white Gloria's Secret terry cloth robe that Gloria had thoughtfully left for me. I towel dried my hair as Blake, with just a towel wrapped dangerously low around his narrow hips, splashed on some GS Men's cologne. It smelled divine—spicy with a hint of vanilla. He glanced at himself in the mirror and ruffled his hand through his wet hair. I guess he wasn't going to blow dry his hair or shave. The extra layer of stubble that surrounded his kissable lips made him even sexier.

"Hey, I'm going to make us some breakfast. Just put on a bathing suit and meet me downstairs."

"Are we going to the beach?"

"That's the plan," he said with a wink.

"I can't wait." I was truly excited. It looked like perfect weather to catch some rays and jump some waves.

After a quick kiss, Blake slipped out of the bathroom. I found an elastic and gathered my damp hair into a ponytail. I brushed my teeth and doused myself with the Gloria's Secret SPF 30 moisturizer that was sitting on the marble counter beside a whole slew of beauty products. Gloria was so generous and thoughtful. I made myself a mental note to send her a handwritten thank-you note when I got home along with a gift. Maybe a picture frame or something cute for the twins.

It was actually good to have a little alone time apart from Blake. I studied my reflection in the mirror and smiled. My complexion glowed. And not just from the long, hot shower. It was deeper than that. I'd never looked so happy. Blake Burns had not only awoken my sexuality, but he'd also lit up my heart. Bradley had never made me feel this way. Our relationship was rooted in friendship and routine. And in the end, deceit. My relationship with Blake was rooted in passion, adventure, and honesty. We were quickly becoming best friends as well as lovers. The deep-seated love I felt for him couldn't be measured or put into words. I so hoped we'd figure out a way to move forward once we settled back to work. Having this gorgeous sex god only a thin wall away from me was daunting. I shuddered at the thought. But as he always said, where there's a will, there's a way.

Back in the bedroom, I donned one of the string bikinis Gloria had given me. The black one. It fit me perfectly, the halter-top exposing my pert breasts just the right amount and the high-cut bottom making my long, lean legs look even longer. I slipped my bare feet into the sparkly flip-flops and, at the last minute, threw on one of Blake's collarless white shirts over my bathing suit.

I could smell the intoxicating scent of him on my body. The high thread count Egyptian cotton felt delicious against my skin. The shirttail trailed to my mid thighs and I left it unbuttoned. Oddly, as sexy as the Gloria's Secret lingerie was, wearing Blake's shirt made me feel sexier. It was as if I was part of him and he was part of me.

The aroma of fresh coffee mixed with something delicious drifted in the air. I inhaled deeply. Breakfast.

My hungry stomach growled.

I galloped downstairs and found Blake in the kitchen. Clad in navy blue swim shorts, he was standing before a built-in grill with his bare back to me, flipping pancakes. There was something so sexy about watching a man cook. Especially someone as sexy as Blake.

I inhaled again through my nose, absorbing the mouthwatering mixture of aromas. "Mmm. Everything smells so good!"

"Hope you like pancakes and sausage," he said as he caught the pancake he'd just flipped on his spatula.

"How do you do that?" I ambled over to him. My shoulder blade rubbed against his flexed bicep.

"It's easy. Let me show you."

He stepped behind me and wrapped his arms around me. Skimming my breasts, he put the spatula into my right hand and slipped it under one of the pancakes. With my wrist in one hand and a breast cupped in the other, he said, "Okay on the count of three, toss the pancake into the air, keep your eyes on it, and the spatula steady just above the grill. Ready?"

I nodded, concentrating on the task at hand. It wasn't easy when he was tweaking my nipple beneath the fabric of my shirt and getting me hot and bothered yet again.

"Good. One . . . two . . . three."

I did as he instructed, and trained my unblinking eyes on the pancake I'd flipped. Bingo! It landed smack on the spatula. "Yes!" I shouted out triumphantly.

"Nice one," replied Blake as he helped me transfer the pancake to a nearby platter. It was stacked with perfectly round golden pancakes.

"Okay, now let's see you do one all by yourself."

"No problemo," I said with an air of smug confidence. *I'll show him.*

But as I shifted the spatula under another pancake, his right hand joined his left on the unoccupied breast. He began to knead them, squeezing and circling. My nipples hardened beneath the fabric of my bikini and sent arousal straight to my core. A hot shiver shot down my spine as I felt his own arousal pressing against my backside. *Oh, God!*

And then one hand slid under my bikini bottom and made a beeline for my clit. That did it. With a loud moan, I flipped the pancake. It went flying and landed two feet away from me on the bleached hardwood floor.

"Fuck!" I wasn't sure if I was reacting to my cooking faux pas or to what was cooking between my legs. Things were heating up quickly. And as if things couldn't get more out of control, I squirmed and accidentally knocked over the bowl of batter. *Crash!* While the ceramic bowl didn't break, a pool of the goo spread all around my feet. Fumbling for the nearby roll of paper towels, I crouched and got down on my hands and knees to clean up the mess I'd made.

"I'm sorry," I groaned, impossibly trying to blotch

up the gooey mess. I saturated one paper towel after another. Why did I have to be Calamity Jen?

"Don't be." I could hear amusement in Blake's voice. "I love seeing a woman on her hands and knees."

"I've totally fucked up breakfast."

"No you haven't. Breakfast is about to be served."

Before I could say a word, Blake hit the floor, and in one smooth move, spread my legs and yanked down my bikini bottoms. Kneeling behind me, my ass raised in the air and legs parted, he penetrated my pussy, inch by delicious inch. I let out a loud moan.

"You've been a bad student," he growled.

"I'm sorry," I squeaked as he began to pound into me from behind. My breasts and ponytail dusted the spilled batter as I rocked my hips to meet his thrusts.

"You need to be punished."

Without warning, I felt a light sting on one of my butt cheeks. I yelped. He slapped me again a little harder. He wasn't using his hand. It was the spatula.

He continued to slap my bottom as he ground into me. The pain mixed with the pleasure. Erotic moans and groans escaped my throat. It felt incredible!

"You like that," he breathed with a deliciously painful yank of my ponytail that lifted my head away the floor.

I simply nodded as my pussy gripped his hot pumping cock. He was hitting my G-spot again and again. I squeezed my eyes shut as my orgasm rose inside me.

Upon another hard yank of my ponytail, I screamed and imploded.

"Fuck!" shouted Blake as his own powerful release met mine. He folded himself on top of me, and after our breathing steadied, lifted me up so I was sitting back on my heels, in his arms.

I pivoted my head around to face him. A mischievous glint flickered in his eyes, and a wicked smile curled on his lips. Holding me in one arm, he dipped a long index finger into the batter and then put it to my lips.

"Suck," he ordered.

"Mmm," I moaned as my mouth curled around his fingertip and savored the sweetness. He licked off the little bit that got on my lips.

"Mmm," he repeated. "You're delicious enough to eat. Turn around and take off my shirt."

I did as he asked, slipping his shirt off my shoulders, and faced him. I studied his features. That maddening mouth was twisted and those blue eyes twinkled with mischief. Oh yeah. Mr. Bad Boy was up to something. In the blink of an eye, he tore off my bikini top and fastened it around my head like a blindfold.

"Blake, I can't see."

"That's the point. Now, don't move," he said as I heard him scramble to his feet.

Every muscle in my body twitched in anticipation

of what was next.

When his warm breath heated my face, I knew he was back on the floor. An unexpected ticklish sensation overtook my senses. He was drizzling a warm liquid on me. He began on my neck, and slowly, the liquid made its way down my chest to my breasts. The sweet familiar smell penetrated my nose. Holy shit. He was dousing me in maple syrup. He circled my nipples with the molten liquid and then let it drip on the tips. My back involuntarily arched and I let out a moan.

"Do you like this?" he purred.

"Oh yes," I purred back.

"You look so edible."

In a heated breath, his velvet lips and tongue were on my breasts, sucking and licking the sweet syrup. Oh God! I could feel my own sweet syrup pooling between my legs.

"This is the best fucking pancake breakfast ever," he murmured into my cleavage after laving it. "And it's only going to get better."

With his mouth still clinging to my tit, he trickled maple syrup down my torso, over my ribs, and then poured it into the pit of my navel. He trailed his tongue slowly down my body, lapping up the syrup. The tip dipped into my navel and flicked the little basin. Oh, God! I never knew how sensitive this part of my body was. Goose bumps exploded across my skin.

"Mmm. You're so fucking delicious," he said

breathily. "Breakfast may be my new favorite meal."

In my mind's eye, I could see the pleasure etched on his face. It was as delicious for me as it was for him. I moaned wordlessly.

"Now, I want to taste your sweet pussy." He spread my legs.

A gasp escaped my lips. And a shiver ran down my spine as the maple syrup dripped down my body and made its way to my quivering pussy. I could feel him pour a generous amount. He used his fingers to spread it across my sensitive folds. It mixed with the sweet syrup that already coated my cleft. I couldn't stop moaning.

Still blindfolded, I felt his warm breath between my legs, heating me. "Oh, baby, you smell so good. So sweet. I'm going to eat you."

My head fell back as the tip of his tongue met my clit.

"Oh yeah," he groaned.

"Oh God, Blake," I moaned. Nothing had prepared me for the touch of his hot, gifted tongue.

The soft flick was followed by fervent laps. Lap after lap. My man was famished. Ravenous for me. Mad with lust. My fingers tangled his damp silky hair as I let him savor the sweetness between my thighs. Lick by sweet lick, the pulsating pressure escalated, driving me to the point of no return. The blindfold only heightened the sensation. My face contorted and my breathing grew ragged. He was devouring me. I thought I was going to jump out of my skin. I honestly couldn't take it anymore.

"You taste so fucking good," Blake murmured, unable to get enough of me.

"Make me come," I cried out.

"You're almost there," he breathed into my throbbing pussy.

He sucked my clit and I came with a scorching roar of his name. Oh. My. God.

Blake drew my trembling body into his arms and whipped off the bikini top from my eyes. Blinking them several times as they adjusted to the light, I soaked him in. A smug, triumphant smile curled on his face.

"Have you had enough of breakfast?" He kissed my lips. I could taste me on him. All sweet and sticky.

"Mmm." I eyed the bottle of maple syrup he'd used on the floor and then my gaze shifted to his crotch. There was a sizable bulge beneath the fabric of his swimsuit. I smiled sheepishly and responded to his question.

"No, Blake. I'm craving some of that sausage. Take off your swim shorts."

His brows shot up and he smiled that sexy crooked smile. "You know, baby, I love a girl with a hearty appetite who understands mine." He quickly did as I asked, and in a few hot breaths, he was kneeling before me, buck naked with his giant cock pointed at me. His smile widened and his daring eyes glimmered.

Still sitting back on my heels, I reached for the syrup and drizzled a drop of it on the crown. Lowering my head, I flicked it with my tongue. His cock jumped.

"Mmm." I licked my lips.

I went back for some more, this time rolling my tongue around the wide rim.

"So good," I moaned as he hissed. Indeed it was—a heady combination of sweet and salty though the sweetness of the syrup prevailed. Blake let out a throaty groan.

I lifted my head and met his gaze. "Blake, I have to tell you something."

His brows arched. "What might that may be?"

"I've always loved sausage swimming in syrup."

Grinning, Blake eyed me shrewdly, knowing damn well where breakfast was heading (no pun intended). "Yeah, that's the way I like it too," he replied as I doused his monstrous length with the thick golden liquid. I ended up using the rest of the bottle.

Dropping my head again, I wrapped my lips around his crown and sucked. So, so, good. "Mmmmmm," I hummed. I was so hungry—and turned on—I could eat him whole.

He let out another moan, this one deeper and louder. "Tiger, take it all." I felt his large hand press on my head, coaxing me to go down on him. Slowly, I dragged my mouth down his rigid shaft, savoring the maple flavor along the way.

"Oh yeah." He hissed again, releasing my head as I made my way back up.

"Harder, deeper," he groaned.

This time I worked my mouth down his hot thick length, dragging my teeth lightly along the pulsing vein, until I could feel the tip tickle the back of my throat.

"Jesus, tiger. That's so fucking good."

His compliment inspired me to repeat the movements and pick up speed. I heard myself humming as I worked his cock fast and furious. My throaty sounds harmonized with his feral groans. His immensity filled the hollows of my cheek and, in no time, I could feel it pulsing inside my mouth. Preparing for orgasm.

"Jen, baby, I'm going to come. Are you ready?"

I nodded as I descended on him one more time. As I took him to the hilt, his organ exploded deep inside my mouth, blasting hot cum down my throat. I squeezed my eyes and swallowed. My mouth stayed clamped on his cock as he slowly pulled out. Lifting my head, I opened my eyes and met his.

"Fuck, tiger, that was the best head I've ever gotten."

I gazed down at his cock. It was still semi-erect, glistening with a combination of cum, saliva, and syrup. Still, so, so edible. My tongue wet my lips.

"My mother always told me to clean my plate. To never leave leftovers," I said as I bent down and licked the delicious remains of our pancake and sausage breakfast. He came again.

He blew out a hot breath. "Your mother taught you well." He lifted my head up by my ponytail and slammed his mouth onto mine.

After breakfast, I wanted to take another shower. We were both so sweaty and sticky. Blake had a better idea. Ten minutes later, after climbing down the steep cliff side stairs that led to a private beach, we were jumping waves in the ocean. Though a competent swimmer, I was somewhat afraid of the ocean. But Blake held me in his strong arms as we navigated the fierce waves. Like always, he made me feel safe. I kissed him many times while waves licked my clit.

After half an hour of frolicking, Blake carried me from the ocean and set me down on the warm, sparkling sand. I was dripping wet, and though the dip was refreshing, I was a little chilled. I was eager to wrap myself in one of the large beach towels we'd brought along.

Drying off, I couldn't help but notice how truly god-like Blake looked. He was so much bigger than me. So much more powerful. Every finely honed muscle glistened in the sunlight, and on his golden skin, specks of the salty sea sparkled like fairy dust. There was something so damn sexy about him with his hair slicked back and his wet-lashed blue eyes glimmering like jewels. I swear, I wanted to jump him.

Running his large hand through his shimmering dark hair, he caught my eyes on him. "Are you staring at me again, tiger?"

I smiled sheepishly and felt myself blush. "I can't help it. Sometimes, Blake, I don't think you're real."

A devilish smile splashed across his face. "Believe me, baby. *I'm* the *real* McCoy.

I felt my towel and bikini fall from me and, in the sound of a crashing wave, I was rolling in the sand with him.

"Are you going to fuck me?" I giggled.

"That's the plan."

"But don't you have ocean dick?" I'd read once that men's organs shriveled in the cold salty water.

He smirked as he shoved off his swim trunks. "That doesn't apply to me."

My eyes widened. No, it didn't. Blake's cock in its full glory was ready for action. I blissfully screamed out his name as he rolled on top of me and plunged it into my pussy. Another first. I was being fucked on the beach. In a bed of sand.

"Does. This. Feel. Real. To. You?" he beat out on each hard, long masterful stroke.

"Yes," I gasped. *So real. So good. So right.*

He continued to ruthlessly pound into me. His

hands were anchored in the sand while mine dug into his muscular flesh. The warmth of the sand beneath me contrasted deliciously with the coolness of his ocean-wet body above me. His eyes shone fierce with passion and determination.

"Do you want it harder, tiger?"

"Oh, yes."

He obliged and grunts accompanied the forceful blows, each so deep it hit my G-spot. His pubic bone rubbed against my clit and my nipples hardened with erotic pleasure from the friction of his chest. The crashing ocean waves sounded in my ears as my own glorious waves began to curl inside me like a tsunami. My shrieks competed with the squawking gulls and Blake's grunts and groans. I was about to have an orgasm of epic proportions.

"Oh, Blake, I'm going to come big time." The words choked out.

"Hold on, baby." On the next deep, powerful thrust, we climaxed together, his massive orgasm riding my sea of fierce waves. Tears leaked from my eyes as he shouted out my name. He collapsed his head onto my breasts as if they were two soft pillows and breathed audibly against them. I ran my fingers through his damp silky hair and caressed his sun-baked back, relishing the warm ripples of his muscles beneath my hand. Tears continued to scroll down my cheeks. Oh, how I loved him—so very much.

We stayed in this position for several long, sensuous minutes, his molten cock buried deep inside me. The music of the sea played in my head as his warm body sheltered me from the cool ocean breeze. I never wanted to lose him, and at the thought, my arms wrapped tightly around him, wanting to hold him forever. I needed to hear him say those three words again. As if he heard my thoughts, he raised his head and gazed into my eyes. He told me he loved me and that I was his tiger. My heart melted as my insecurity lifted. I had to stop thinking I might lose him or he would hurt me. He doused me with kisses and my worries dissipated.

Slowly, he pulled out of me and rolled off my body. "Stay there," he ordered. "You look so beautiful. I want to take some photos."

I bolted to a sitting position. My body was covered with sand from head to toe. I tried to fix my damp sandy ponytail. It was futile.

"Blake, no! I look terrible." I hastily brushed off some of the sand and smoothed my hair.

"Trust me, you look beautiful," he responded as he bent down to retrieve his iPhone on the beach blanket we'd brought along. He sat back down, cross-legged, beside me.

"Let's take some selfies."

"No," I protested again. "I'm a mess."

"You look perfect." He drew me into his arms and

playfully kissed my lips as he held up his phone. *Click.*
"Now smile." *Click.* I pecked him on the cheek. *Click.*
"Make a funny face." We both stuck out our tongues.
Click. Our tongues met. *Click.* And we kissed again.

After the hot open-mouthed kiss, Blake insisted on
taking some solo pictures of me.

"As long as I'm not naked. Just my face."

"Promise. Scout's Honor." With his free hand, he
gave me the three-finger hand signal and then squatted
in front of me.

I shot him a playful dirty look. "You were never a
Boy Scout!"

"Nope. Scout's Honor," he laughed as he clicked
away.

After a dozen or so shots, I begged to see the photos—just to be sure Mr. Bad Boy wasn't shooting me
nude. Before he could say a word, I snatched the phone
out of his hand and pressed the camera roll. A barrage
of snapshots filled the screen. My eyes popped, and my
heart did a flip-flop landing hard in my chest. Shaking,
I clicked onto the photo I couldn't get my eyes off. The
phone was muted, but I didn't need sound. My mouth
fell open as I watched a video that Blake had taken. The
video of Bradley and his hygienist, Candace, groping at
each other in a heated embrace. Close to hyperventilat-
ing, my heart raced and my breathing labored. Blake's
voice hacked into my state of shock.

"See, baby, you can trust me."

I stopped the video—I didn't need to see it to the end—and finally got my mouth to move. "How could you?"

"What are you talking about?"

"*You* took that video of Bradley all over his hygienist and sent it to me? *You're* Charles Palmer the third?"

Squeezing his eyes shut, Blake flung his head back and muttered three words. "Fuck. Fuck. Fuck."

"Fuck you!" Tears of rage welled up in my eyes. "How could you do that to me?"

Blake ran a hand through his hair and sucked in a gulp of air. "Baby, I wanted to save you."

"Save me?" My quivering voice had risen an octave. "Save me from the first man I loved? The man I was going to marry?" I shook my head as tears streamed down my face. "No, you wanted to destroy him."

"You deserved better."

I swiped at my tears. "Oh, yeah? Someone better? Like some bastard like you?"

"Jennifer, I didn't mean to hurt you. Honestly."

"Well, you did, you deceitful, conniving bastard." I clambered to put my bathing suit back on. "Here . . . take your fucking phone. I'm out of here." Rising to my feet, I hurled the phone at him. He managed to catch it as I stormed off.

"Wait!"

"Don't you dare follow me!" I shouted without

turning to look at him.

With blinding tears, I plodded through the warm sand as quickly as I could, my feet sinking deeply into the sparkling granules. Dark thoughts bombarded my mind. What sick fuck would do something like that? How could I fall for someone like that? And how was I ever going to work for him? The ocean breeze sent a chill up my spine as hot tears scorched my face. I needed to get out here and clear my head. Pack up my stuff and call for a Lip Service car. Yes, that's what I would do.

My calves ached from running in the sand, but the sooner I could get out of here, away from the bastard, the better. Not far from the steep cliff side stairway that led up to Gloria and Jaime's glass palace, a sharp pain stabbed at my right foot. Yelping a loud "ow,' I stopped dead in my tracks and winced as the piercing pain radiated up my leg. Balancing on my left leg, I examined the sole of my other foot. Fuck. I'd stepped on a piece of glass, and the three-inch shard was lodged deep in my arch. Without over thinking, I squeezed my eyes and yanked it out. Tears spilled down my face as I let out a loud shriek of pain. Clutching the shard, I surveyed the damage. I was left with a deep, jagged gash; blood gushed out as nausea rose to my chest. I was never good with blood. Lowering my foot to the sand, I tippytoed so as not to get sand in the wound. The location of the cut made that impossible. I tried walking on my heel; that didn't work either. I pondered my next move as blood soaked the sparkling grains. When I heard Blake calling out to me and getting closer, I picked up my pace. I tried putting my foot down, but the pain was too much. I almost buckled. Lifting my heel back up, I forced myself to keep going. The bleeding got worse, and a lightheaded feeling set in.

"Jen!"

Before I could take another agonizing step, two strong hands gripped my shoulders, holding me back. Blake.

"Let go of me," I screamed through my tears. To my relief, he released me, and I hobbled away. I groaned with each step. The pain was unbearable.

Blake trailed behind me. "What's wrong? Why are you limping?"

"I stepped on a piece of glass," I blurted, not slowing down. My tears were blurring my vision, and the blood loss was taking its toll. I was a walking disaster. Losing stamina, I stumbled. Just before I hit the sand, Blake caught me. His strong arm clamped my waist.

"Let me see your foot." Reluctantly, I lifted my foot to show him the damage.

"Hold onto my shoulder for a minute." I moved my hand to his broad shoulder. As I gripped it and suppressed a moan, he crouched down and examined my wound.

"Jesus. That's really deep." I peeked at my foot and shuddered. It looked liked some kindergartener had smeared a jar of red finger paint all over it. It was a throbbing, bloody mess.

"You're going to need to get stitches."

"The only thing I need is to get away from you," I snapped back at him.

"I'll take you home after I take you to an emergency room. That cut's going to get infected if it's not treated properly."

"Leave me alone." I choked out the words, my physical and emotional strength dwindling. I tried to put pressure on my foot, but it was futile. I gazed woefully at the daunting cliff side stairs ahead of me. How was I going to make it up all those steep, jagged steps? There must have been a hundred of them. Maybe more.

"Climb onto my back," Blake commanded, still squatting. "Or you're going to bleed to death right here."

I was going to die? In my head, I fantasized the headline in *The Hollywood Reporter:* "Aspiring Porn Producer Found Dead at Famed Malibu Residence." Subtitle: "Cause of Death Being Investigated." Blake's voice hurled me back to reality.

"Just fucking do it!" He sounded frustrated and desperate.

There was no way I was going to make it up those

steps. I had no choice. Holding on to him for balance, I hopped behind him and then mounted him, curling my legs around his waist and wrapping my arms around his shoulders. He stood up.

"Hold on," he ordered as he began to trudge through the sand with me on his back, piggyback style. I tightened my grip around him as if my life depended on it. Because it did. His rippled muscles brushed against my chest, and I could feel his chest rise and fall with every step. Huge drops of blood dotted the sand, leaving a trail behind us as we forged ahead.

I don't know how he did it—probably thanks to climbing all those steps at the Santa Monica Stairs—but he got us up the impossible cliff side, Step by steep step. He wasn't even out of breath when we got to the top. He was obviously in top shape from working out so much. He gently deposited me onto of one of the cushioned wicker rocking chairs on the deck. I noticed for the first time that I'd gotten blood all over his swim shorts and there were traces of it down the side of his muscular leg as well.

Blood quickly puddled on the wood planks. While I silently freaked, Blake grabbed the towel that was draped over the back of the chair and told me to press it against the open wound.

Leaning forward, I crossed my injured leg over my other knee, and did as he asked. Shit. It hurt.

"Wait right here. I'll be right back," he said, dashing into the house.

Believe me, I was going nowhere. I was in no condition to walk even if I could. The loss of blood had
made me woozy. I felt faint and was thankful to be
resting in the comfortable chair. Remembering I was
still holding the fragment of glass in my other hand, I
set it on the small round table next to me. At least, no
one would step on it again.

Blake was back in no time with a tray of first aid. A
box of Gloria's Secret Band-Aids, a bottle of peroxide,
and a clean washcloth. Setting it on the table, he got
down on his knees. He removed the bloodstained towel
and examined my foot. Blood trickled onto his thighs,
but he seemed oblivious.

His brows furrowed. "This is going to sting," he
said softly as he soaked the washcloth with the
peroxide. Holding my ankle, he dabbed the moistened
cloth on the laceration.

I yelped and almost leapt out of the wicker chair.
"What the fuck are you doing? Haven't you hurt me
enough?"

His eyes stayed focused on my foot. "I need to
clean this up. Get the sand off."

I bit down on my bottom lip as he attended to the
gash. The expression on his face was intense. After a
few more dabs, he tossed the blood-soaked cloth onto
the deck and tore opened the Band-Aid box. Frantically,
one by one, he ripped open the plastic bandages with

his teeth and pasted them over my open cut. They were white with little hot pink hearts in the center. He must have gone through entire box because a mountain of wrappers sat on the deck. There wasn't a single one left for my broken heart.

His forehead creased as he inspected his handiwork. "Fuck. This isn't working. You're bleeding right through all the Band-Aids. Don't move. I'll be right back again."

He quickly returned. This time with another dry white towel in one hand and a leather belt in the other. One of the floral sundresses Gloria had gifted me was draped over his sculpted forearm. Crouching, he hastily folded the towel up into a thick six-inch square and pressed it hard against my bleeding wound.

Another loud gasp of pain escaped my throat. His gaze met my tearing eyes.

"I'm sorry. I didn't mean to hurt you."

I found it bitterly ironic that he'd just repeated the words he'd said in a different context just a short while ago. I didn't know what hurt more . . . the wound to the sole of my foot or the wound to the soul of my heart. One shed blood; the other bled tears.

I watched as he strapped the leather belt around the makeshift bandage and my foot.

"What are you doing?" I asked, my voice nothing more than a hoarse whisper.

"Making a tourniquet to stop the bleeding."

"Where'd you learn to do that?"

"Boy Scouts."

I almost snorted, but he handed me the floral sundress before I could utter a sound.

"I thought you might want to put this on. Do you need any help?" His forlorn eyes searched mine.

"No." After my snippy one-word reply, I slipped the dress over my head and my two arms through the spaghetti straps. I shimmied the skirt of the dress past my thighs. Though the temperature was mild, I began to shiver. The loss of blood was wreaking havoc on my body. I felt cold, broken, and empty. Teeth chattering, I folded my arms across my chest.

"Geez. You're fucking freezing," breathed out Blake. Not wasting a second, he grabbed an ocean-blue afghan folded over an adjacent chaise and wrapped it around me. The next thing I knew, I was in his arms, cradled like a baby.

"There's an urgent care center a few miles down on PCH. We'll be there in no time."

Wearily, I rested my head against his chest as we headed to his car. I wanted no part of him, yet here I was all his.

Chapter 13

Blake

It took us a short fifteen minutes to get to the urgent care center. The drive had been as painful for me as it was for her. We were steeped in cold silence, fighting our emotions. Jennifer kept her pale face turned away from me, staring out at the ocean on her right. I wondered what was going through her mind. For sure, nothing good. What had started out as a glorious romantic weekend had ended up in disaster.

I parked my car in the first spot available outside the cookie cutter cement structure. There were only a few other cars, all parked in reserved spaces—obviously for the doctors, nurses, and paramedics who worked here. It appeared we were the only ones here with a New Year's Day emergency. I hopped out of the car and rounded it to help Jen out of her seat and carry her into the center.

"What can I do for you?" asked a plump redheaded receptionist. Smoothing her Minnie Mouse print nurse's smock, she eyed Jennifer. "Food poisoning? There's been a lot of that going around. People must be eating some bad fish."

"No. My girlfr—" I stopped myself just in time. "She stepped on a piece of glass; I think she needs stitches."

The receptionist lowered her eyes to Jennifer's foot. "We get a lot of that too. Damn those bums who litter our beaches."

It was unlikely that a bum—or anyone for that matter—had been trespassing on the Zanders's private beachfront property. Most likely, the glass had gotten there during the construction of their house. It wasn't, however, worth explaining to this pigheaded woman.

"She needs to fill out some forms. I assume she has insurance."

"Yes. " Jennifer nodded.

The receptionist pulled out a clipboard with some forms and a pen attached to it. She stood up and handed it to Jennifer. "Take a seat somewhere, and when you're done filling out the paperwork, I'll call someone to wheel you back to see the doctor on duty."

Jennifer quirked a faint smile. I got us settled into two armchairs. She kept her foot up on the coffee table in front of us as she filled out the forms.

"Done," said Jennifer. Obviously, the lazy receptionist bitch wasn't going to leave her throne, so I took the liberty of handing them over to her. She perused them quickly and then called for a wheelchair. An attendant arrived right away, pushing one. I helped

Jennifer stand up and situate herself in the chair.

"Do you want me to come with you?" I asked.

"I want you to leave." Her voice was as cold as dry ice.

My heart ached as she was wheeled away. There was no way I was leaving her here by herself, whether she liked it or not. I sunk back into my chair and pulled out my iPhone to check my e-mails and texts. But there was something I needed to do first. Delete the video. With an indignant press of my finger, I made it disappear.

Fuck this phone! Fuck *Operation Dickwick!* How could I have been so stupid to have not erased the video? Stupid, stupid me. Maybe what made me fucking stupid in the first place was taking it. Sending it to her under a false identity was a shit-ass thing to do. I wasn't just fucking stupid. I was a fucking stupid asshole! I'd fucked up big time. I'd succeeded in prying her away from Dickwick, but now I was the dick with a price to pay. I knew she'd never want to see me again, and I had no clue how we were going to work together. Was she going to say good-bye to her job as well?

While Jennifer was being treated, I beat up on myself. I had no solution to the damage I'd caused. Sorry. I didn't mean to hurt you wasn't going to cut it. Not with someone like Jennifer. I was going to be her forever bastard.

Forty-five long minutes and twenty stitches later,

Jennifer re-emerged from the emergency room. Her foot was mummified in bandages, and she was on crutches. I stood up as she hobbled my way. Her face was still pale and pained.

"I'll take you home," I said quietly, longing to take her into my arms, crutches and all.

"No need. I had a nurse call Lip Service. A car should be here any minute."

I was taken aback. "Are you sure? Seriously, it's not out of my way."

"There's no discussion." Her voice was still frosty.

"At least let me pay for it," I pleaded.

"No need," she repeated. "I put it on my credit card."

A heavyset foreign-looking man entered through the automatic doors.

"Ms. McCoy?" he asked, searching Jennifer's forlorn eyes. Obviously, he was the Lip Service dude.

Jennifer nodded and followed him out, struggling on her crutches. My eyes never left her, the crutches and bandage a reminder of all the pain I had caused her. Goddamn it. For the first time in my life, I hated myself.

Chapter 14

Jennifer

Thank goodness, I had a Lip Service account—an online alternative taxi service that was quickly becoming one of he best ways to get around in LA if you didn't have a car or were unable to drive one. My credit card was on file. I made it home.

"What the fuck happened to you?" asked Libby, her eyes wide, as I stood at the front door on my crutches. It was just a little after five. It was a good thing she was home because I'd left my bag with my wallet and keys at the beach house. She continued to rant.

"And why haven't I heard from you? When did you get back from Boise?"

In retrospect, I should have let Libby know what was happening. I hadn't spoken or texted her during the break. I took a deep breath.

"I have a lot to tell you," I muttered as I hobbled into the living room. I still hadn't quite gotten the hang of getting around on crutches, and they moreover made my armpits ache. Fortunately, the kindly doctor who had stitched up my foot said I would only need to be on them for a week. By then, the pain would subside and there would be little chance for infection, as long as I kept the gash well covered.

I collapsed onto the couch, leaning my crutches against the armrest. I propped my bandaged foot on the coffee table, remembering the doctor wanted me to keep it elevated as much as possible for the next twenty-four hours. I reached for one of the decorative pillows gracing the couch, but Libby got to it before me.

"Here, let me help you," she said, placing the pillow under my heel. I couldn't ask for a better best friend than Libby.

"Anything else I can do?"

"A glass of wine would be great." I rarely drank before six o'clock, but today warranted an exception. My head was pounding with sorrow and regret.

"You got it." My bestie scurried out of the room and returned quickly with two glasses of white wine, one for her, one for me.

After handing me a glass, Libby sunk into her favorite armchair. "Now tell me everything."

So much had gone down in the last week, I didn't know where to begin. After a sip of the chilled wine, I tearfully blurted out, "Blake Burns and I fell in love, and now it's over."

Libby's eyes practically popped out of their sockets and her jaw dropped to the floor. I'd never seen her so stunned. "Are you fucking kidding me?"

I shook my head.

"Why didn't you tell me?"

"I don't know, Lib. I'm sorry. It all just happened so fast."

She glanced down at my bandaged foot. "Rough sex?"

I shook my head again. "No, rough weekend."

"Well, you'd better start explaining."

With a heavy sigh, I took a long sip of my wine and started from the beginning. How Blake Burns was the man I'd kissed and fallen for when I'd play that game of Truth or Dare, blindfolded, on the night of my engagement party.

Libby gulped her wine and fluttered her eyes with shock. "Holy Fuck! How did you find out?"

I told her about the kiss under the mistletoe at the office party and then how we'd fucked our brains out in his fuck pad.

"Holy Shit!" She guzzled her wine. "I may have to open another bottle. Keep talking."

I told her about everything that had happened back home—his surprise visit, his declaration of love, our first night together in my bedroom, and even our enchanted fuck in the snow. Rivulets of tears poured down my face as I recounted and relived all these magical moments.

Libby was all ears. "Wow! I hate to admit it, but he

sounds amazing. I don't get it. What happened?"

Skimming over the Springer stuff, I launched into our New Year's weekend in Malibu. I could no longer hold back. I burst into hysterical sobs. "Libby, he did something terrible."

She eyed my bandaged foot and her eyes widened. "He hurt you?"

I nodded. "He hurt me. But not physically." I took a break to brush away my tears. "Libby, I found out he was the one who took and sent that video of Bradley and Candace." I tearfully told her how.

Libby gasped. "No way. I mean, I never liked Bradley, but that's totally creepy. What a fucking lowlife bastard!"

"I know. I couldn't believe it. I split as fast I could but stepped on a piece of glass." I adjusted my bandaged foot on the pillow. "Twenty fucking stitches."

"You poor thing," consoled Libby as she reached to dab my tears with a paper cocktail napkin. "I can't believe this has all happened."

"Lib, you've got to promise not to tell anyone at work about Blake and me."

"I promise." My big-mouthed friend glanced down again at my foot. "Does your foot hurt?"

"Right now, it's numb. The doctor gave me some painkillers. I probably shouldn't be drinking, but fuck it."

"What are you going to do about Blake?"

I bit down on my lip. "I don't want to see him again."

"What about your job?"

I heaved a breath. That was the big question. How could I continue to work with the bastard? Face him every day? Deal with the pain? Get through the rage? Yet, I loved my job. And wanted so badly to see the block of women's programming I was developing come to fruition. Fuck, what was I going to do? I was too hurt and confused to think straight. I swiped at my tears and shrugged my shoulders.

"I don't know, Lib. What would you do?" I croaked, my voice hoarse. "No one from Nick or Disney is going to hire me with SIN-TV on my resumé."

My friend, the analyst, knitted her unruly brows in deep thought. "Don't quit. It's a great job and you're doing great things. The company is going to recognize you. And when they do, you'll be able to move up wherever you want. So, I know it's going to be hard, but hang in there."

I digested Libby's words. She was right as usual. Except it wasn't going to be hard to hang in there. It was going to be next to impossible. I sipped more wine.

A loud knock-knock-knock at the front door caught us both by surprise. Puzzled, Libby jumped up from her chair and headed toward it. "Did you order a pizza?" I asked as she peered through the peephole.

Not answering me, she unbolted the door and bent down to retrieve something. Slamming the door closed, she stood up and turned to face me. Two familiar objects were dangling from her hands: My purse and my suitcase. And tucked under an arm was Blake's white tiger.

My mouth fell open and my heart thudded. "Is he out there?"

Libby shook her head. "I saw him drive off."

I sighed with relief, yet a dagger of disappointment dug into my gut. My stomach twisted painfully.

Grabbing my crutches, I lifted myself off the couch. My foot throbbed. The pain medicine the doctor had given me must be wearing off. Maybe later, Libby would go out and pick up the prescription the doctor called in for me at our local CVS. Yes. That's what I needed. Pain pills. They might alleviate the pain in my foot, but the pain in my heart was mine to bear.

I hopped in the direction of my bedroom. "Lib, could you do me a big favor and bring my things to my room?"

"Sure," my bestie said brightly. Wheeling the suitcase, she followed me down the narrow hallway that led to my room.

"Where do you want everything?" she asked.

"On my bed would be fine."

She complied. "Cute tiger," she said as she propped it against my pillow. "A Christmas present from your parents?"

"Yes," I stuttered. For some reason, I didn't want to share the fact it was from Blake. Fighting back tears, I eyed the plush toy wistfully. And then I glanced down at my chest. A little gasp escaped my throat. I was missing the pendant necklace with the tourmaline heart that Blake had given me along with the tiger. I must have lost it in the ocean or maybe the sand. Another wave of sadness swept over me. It stood for everything that was Blake. Everything that *was* us. Something rare and beautiful. And now, it was forever gone.

I was on the verge of crying when Libby's voice sounded. "Want me to help you unpack?"

"Thanks, but I think I can manage." My room was small, so it wouldn't be that big a deal to hang up the stuff I'd brought to Boise or tuck it away in my armoire. Even on crutches. I probably could just hop around on one foot and use a single crutch for support if I had to. Plus, I needed some alone time.

"Is there anything else you need me to do?" There was genuine compassion in Libby's voice.

With a tearful voice, I asked if she could bring me some saran wrap or a plastic garbage bag so I could wrap my foot up and take a much needed shower; I was still covered all over with sand and salt. I also asked if she didn't mind going to the pharmacy to pick up my pain pills. I was quickly discovering that being on crutches was ridiculously humbling. Lucky for me, my best friend couldn't be more obliging. God, I loved Libby!

When Libby returned with a roll of saran wrap, I thanked her and asked her a few questions about her holiday, realizing I'd so selfishly only talked about myself. She told me she'd had a relaxing week and a blast at the *Chorus Line*-themed New Year's Eve party her twin brother Chaz had thrown. Eager to get to the pharmacy before it closed, she told me she'd tell me more when she got back. After a hug, she took off to pick up my meds as well as some Chinese take-out. It didn't matter to me what kind of food she brought back. Nauseated and terribly saddened, I had no appetite.

I decided to take a shower first. After securely wrapping up my bandaged foot with the entire roll of saran wrap, I hobbled down the hall to the bathroom we shared. Luckily, we had a stall shower that was easy to step into, and it even had a handicap rail left behind by the elderly tenant who'd inhabited this house before us.

I debated whether I should take my crutches into the shower, but ultimately left them against the glass shower door. On one foot, I hopped into the shower and turned it on.

Holding on to the handicap rail, my bad foot raised, I let the hot water pound on my head. I soaped up the large sponge and began to wash the memories of today away. Granules of sand laced the tiled floor. I softly brushed the sponge over my breasts and then moved it to the delicate folds between my legs. I couldn't wash the throbbing away. Damn it! He was still with me. The memory of taking a shower with Blake this morning filled my head. How sensual it had been—first that mind-blowing finger fuck and then fucking me against the wall in a steamy haze until I fell apart. I could feel him now. His mouth on my wet flesh, his magnificent cock thrusting against my own wet walls, my pussy throbbing. My breathing grew shallow. I was masturbating, rubbing the sponge against my clit to bring myself to a climax of despair. Tears seared my eyes as I came.

Hastily, I washed my hair. The scent of the shampoo aroused yet more memories. The Very Cherry Vanilla shampoo was from Gloria's Secret. A little got in my eyes. It stung like the memories the shampoo brought back.

Not bothering to condition my hair, I carefully hopped out of the shower. After towel drying myself, I wrapped myself in the fluffy bathrobe I always kept on a nearby hook, and then palmed the shower door for balance as I removed the saran wrap from my injured foot. Success. The bandage had remained dry. But the throbbing in my foot had intensified. I hoped Libby would hurry back soon with my meds.

I grabbed my crutches and hobbled over to the sink. I glanced at myself in the mirror. My reflection shocked me. Even after the shower, I looked drawn and drained. My eyes were swollen-red and my lips puffy—all from crying. Fuck *that* man! He had turned me into a heartbroken, blubbering mess. With more tears threatening to fall, I quickly brushed my hair and teeth and headed back to my room.

I was beat, physically and emotionally. And my foot hurt like fucking hell. But I was determined to unpack. To put away the memories of today once and for all. I lowered myself to my bed, leaning the crutches against it, and zipped open my suitcase. My eyes widened and my heart stammered. Neatly packed on top of my belongings was all the Gloria's Secret lingerie I'd worn with Blake. And there was something else—Blake's collarless shirt. I reached for the shirt and put it to my nose. It smelled of him. It smelled of me. It smelled of us.

Except there was no more us. I flung the shirt to the floor as if it were toxic. Fuck *that* man! Fuck that beautiful bastard! He was just trying to get to me. Rage consumed me. With all the muscle strength I could muster, I hurled the bag off the bed. The contents sprawled all over the floor. My room looked as if it had been ransacked by a burglar.

The truth was, I had been robbed. Robbed of my heart. Wrapped in my robe, I curled up on my bed and began to sob. I was almost glad I didn't have my meds because the intense pain in my foot was the only thing that kept the pain in my heart at bay. Clutching the soft white cuddly tiger, I cried myself to sleep.

Chapter 15

Blake

I didn't expect Jennifer to show up at the office. In fact, I was surprised I showed up. After dropping her bags off last night, I had gone to some seedy Hollywood bar where no one knew me and drunk myself to oblivion while some skinny, shaggy, out-of-work musician sang Passenger's "Let Her Go." After the third whisky, I'd stopped counting. I don't know how I got home. I couldn't remember. Amazingly, I wasn't stopped by some cop and hadn't gotten into some head-on collision. The minute I got home, I'd puked my guts out. I was lucky I'd made it to the toilet in time. Vaguely, I remembered collapsing onto my bed without undressing. This morning I was paying the price of my fucked-upness. I had a raging headache; waves of nausea still swarmed my chest, and I looked like shit—eyes bloodshot, hair disheveled, face stubbled. And worse, I felt like a dick. A fucking prick. A stupid bastard. A goddamn asshole. I was the Dickwick, not Bradley Wick, DDS.

No girl had ever walked away from me. I was a

player. I was the one who did the walking. But Jennifer McCoy was no ordinary girl. She had made me feel things I'd never felt before. She'd showed me my heart wasn't just an organ for pumping blood to my cock. It was something more—a home. A home for love. But now, my heart was vacant. The lights were out.

I'd fallen hard in love with Jennifer and I'd stupidly, selfishly fucked it up. In all my almost thirty years, I'd never before had a moment of self-loathing. I'd gotten everything I'd wanted. Done everything I'd wanted to do. Never had a regret. But now, self-loathing ran deep through my veins, darkening my already black heart. I fucking hated myself for what I had done.

Nursing my headache, I was drinking black coffee at my desk and about to boot up my computer when Jennifer hobbled into my office, still on her crutches and wearing the backpack her parents had given her. She looked somber in all black—a full calf-length skirt, a simple black tee, and a pair, or rather, a single ballet flat on her good foot. Her eyes were swollen and red-rimmed behind her glasses, her skin paler than usual. A new wave of nausea swelled inside my chest. Her frail state made me feel even sicker to my stomach.

"Take a seat," I managed, setting down my coffee.

"No need. I won't be staying long."

My heart stuttered. "You've come here to resign?"

She adjusted her crutches and met my gaze. "I've

come here to do my job. I'll be working all day on my Gloria's Secret PowerPoint presentation."

I floundered for words. "How's your foot?"

Her eyes sliced into me like razor blades. "It hurts." With that, she hobbled out of my office, leaving me the stupid prick I was.

I spent the rest of the morning answering e-mails and watching dailies of a new porn flick we were shooting that was scheduled to air in the Fall. Usually, I got a boner watching some dude massage his nine-inch dick between the planet-sized tits of some blond bimbo, but today, I didn't. I could barely focus. And my cock was comatose. My mind was totally consumed by Jennifer. I had the burning urge to burst into her office, sweep her off her feet, and shower her with make-up kisses. The fact that she couldn't walk away made it even more tempting.

Just as the clip of the porn flick ended, my cell phone rang. I glanced down at the caller ID screen. It was Jaime Zander. Fuck. I hadn't even called or e-mailed him to thank him for letting me use his beach house. I had to admit it. I was a prick of epic proportions.

"Yo, Blakeman, how did it go?"

"I fucked up."

"What do you mean?"

I told him about the video. Then, I told him what had happened.

"Jesus. You really did fuck up."

"Jay-Z, why don't you meet me for lunch at Factor's? I could use some cheering up."

"Man, I can't. I'm still in Hawaii. I won't be back till the end of week. I'm flying to Asia tomorrow for business."

Fuck. In the background, I could hear one of the babies crying.

"What should I do?"

"Don't give up on her."

I digested his words. Jaime had deceived Gloria for her own good, too, and had almost lost her. And then he came to her rescue. But this was different.

The crying in the background grew louder. I could hear Gloria telling my best bud to get off the phone.

"Listen, I've gotta go. Call me if you need to talk, pal. Good luck."

We ended the call. I was going to need all the luck in the world to win back my wounded tiger.

Chapter 16

Jennifer

The Kiss. That was the first thing I saw when I'd hobbled into my office—the magnificent painting Blake had given me for Christmas. Before leaving for Boise, I'd had someone from maintenance hang it on the wall.

Debilitated as I was, I wasn't prepared for my reaction. My aching heart almost went into cardiac arrest and my good leg went weak. All at once, every memory associated with that painting bombarded my brain. Each one more beautiful and gut-wrenching than the one before. Unwanted tears—hadn't I cried enough?—spilled from my eyes. God fucking damn it. Blake was back in my bloodstream and knocking at my heart. Places he no longer belonged. I steadied myself on my crutches and tried impossibly hard to will him away. He was toxic. I was stricken by his poison. When I finally managed to settle at my desk, I composed an e-mail to maintenance, asking someone to come by and take the painting down. What was I was going to do with it? Tears flew onto my keyboard as I cluelessly typed.

About to hit "send," I deleted it instead. Sobs shook my body. Thank goodness, the door to my office was closed. I was a confused, tormented, blubbering mess.

I seriously don't know how I made it through the next couple of days. I woke up, went to work, came home, did more work, and then cried myself to sleep. My parents, of course, called me right away, eager to hear how things were going with Blake. Just the mention of his name had my eyes welling with tears. Fighting back the waterworks, I lied and told them that New Year's was fun and everything was going "just great." I knew if I told them what had happened, they'd freak and be on the first plane to LA. As much as I craved a hug from my mom and another from my dad, I needed time to sort through my emotions and gain some form of composure.

"Honey, you don't sound like yourself," commented my perceptive, overprotective mother.

"I'm just tired, Mom," I replied. "I'm working very hard on a presentation. If you don't hear from me this week, that's why." With an exchange of "I love you," we ended the call. The tears that were threatening trickled down my face. Blake had promised my father he wouldn't hurt me, but he had.

I couldn't snap out of my depression. I had restless nights and barely ate a thing. By Wednesday, I noticed my skirts were getting loose on me. I was losing weight, something I didn't need to do. Libby was concerned about my well-being and offered to take me out for dinner with Chaz night after night. I declined, telling her that I had too much work. That was partly the truth, but there was more. I just couldn't. I wasn't in the mood and I would be terrible company. What a shit way to start the New Year. I was fucking miserable.

Being on crutches didn't help either. Everything was a challenge—even the smallest things. The only good thing about them was everyone was so nice to me. At the office, co-workers opened doors for me as well as offered to bring me lunch and even take me back and forth from work. Fortunately, Libby was able to do the latter. She was a total saint.

I immersed myself in my work, avoiding Blake as much as possible. I spent as much time as possible in my office, behind a closed door, developing my erotic daytime block and working on my PowerPoint presentation for my upcoming meeting with Gloria Zander. I really wanted to woo her and get Gloria's Secret on board. I couldn't blow it.

Whenever I could, I e-mailed Blake so I didn't have to see him. When I was summoned to his office, I sat on the couch far away from him. Both of us refrained from eye contact as well as from calling each other by our first names. I was Ms. McCoy; he, Mr. Burns. I said as little as possible, responding to his questions about my projects with a few monotone words. Whenever I stepped into his office or passed by him in the hall, the temperature in the air dropped and my stomach twisted into a painful knot. He avoided me as much as I avoided him.

On Wednesday afternoon, I managed to get out of the office at lunchtime. Libby gave me a lift to Century City where I was going to Bloomingdale's while she met with a research supplier. No matter what had happened at her house, I still wanted to get Gloria Zander a gift to thank her for her generosity before our meeting.

Suddenly ravenous from not having eaten much all week, I headed first to the food court for a quick bite. I longed for something comforting like chicken soup, but ended up with a bowl of hot and sour soup from Panda Express. One of the workers was kind enough to bring my tray to a table. It never ceased to amaze me how much goodwill I'd discovered disabled on crutches.

The piping hot soup was tasty though zingy. Both my stomach and heart were grateful for a little nourishment. As I lifted another spoonful to my mouth, a familiar voice sounded in my ear.

"Bubala!"

I looked up. It was Blake's silver-haired grandma. She sprightly headed my way. She was wearing a soft blue jogging outfit and was in amazing shape for a woman her age. She plunked herself down on the empty chair across from me. Her eyes stayed riveted on my crutches, which were leaning against the table.

"*Oy! Vhat* happened?"

"Just little accident," I said hesitantly.

A sly smile, that reminded me so much of Blake's, splayed across her crinkly face.

"Skiing with my Blakela?" She winked. "Or a little rough *shtumping?*"

Speechless, I cringed. She knew about Blake and me.

"Blakela is *meshuganah* about you."

I plastered a fake smile on my face. I wasn't quite sure what *meshuganah* meant. "I feel the same way," I said tentatively.

She blew an air kiss. "Finally, my gorgeous grandson has found a beautiful *hamishah* girl to marry."

As much as I adored Blake's theatrical grandma, I was falling apart at the seams. I needed to get away from her. But she wouldn't let me. She pressed her bony, veined hand on mine, holding me prisoner. I couldn't break away and hurt the sweet woman's feelings. She continued to rave about Blake.

"Such a good boy! And *vhat* a *shmekel!*"

Every nerve in my body buzzed. Desperate for words, I asked what she was doing here.

"I meet here every *veek* with my erotica book club. *Alvays*, they're late. Too much Botox *shmotox!*"

Despite my anxiety, I had to stifle a little laugh. Blake's grandma loved to read erotic romances and was one of the first to support my idea of creating a SIN-TV block of programming targeted at women—turning top-selling, hot novels into compelling *telenovelas.*

"So, *bubala, ve're* running out of books. Can you recommend something?"

I thought for a moment. "*Blind Obsesssion* by Ella Frank. It's beautifully written and highly erotic."

Her gray-blue eyes lit up. "So it's got a lot of sexy *shmexy?"*

"Yes." I nodded. I just didn't tell her it was very sad. Not every story ended with happily ever after.

I felt my eyes watering. "Nice to see you. I have to run an errand."

She stood up and came around the table to give me a warm hug.

"So, *boobie,* I'll see you Friday night at Shabbat?"

"Y-yes." *No. Not then. Not ever.* Every vivid moment of that first night with Blake danced in my head. How he'd held me in his arms as I anxiously lit the candles. How I'd accidentally found him jerking himself off. How I'd almost peed in my pants when I saw his cock for the very first time. How I'd imagined wrapping my lips around his succulent balls when I put that matzo ball to my mouth. How I'd felt his heat seated next to him. And my own rise between my legs. There was no denying it. I was already in love with him.

Grabbing my crutches, I bid Grandma good-bye and hobbled away before tears betrayed me.

The Bloomingdale's housewares department, located on the store's upper level, was moderately busy. I noticed a number of young women wandering around, with their iPhones or iPads, taking photos of china, crystal, and other home basics. Definitely brides-to-be sorting out their registries. A pang of sadness stabbed at my heart. Perhaps, if Blake hadn't taken that vapid video, I would have been among them. *The Almost Bride*. That was me. What a perfect name for a movie.

I hopped around the display tables in search of the perfect gift for Gloria. Nothing stood out.

"Can I help you?" came a throaty voice from behind me as I admired a silver picture frame that was way out of my price range. A prim, fifty-something saleswoman, who looked like she used every penny of her sales commissions on hair dye and fillers, strode up to me. I flashed her a small smile as she eyed my bandaged foot. I hoped she wasn't going to ask me what happened. Fortunately, she didn't.

"Yes, I'm looking for a thank-you gift. Preferably something with a nautical or marine feeling to it."

"How much do wish to spend?"

I told her my price range was between thirty and fifty dollars.

She winked and raised a knowing forefinger. "I

know the perfect item." Glancing down at my foot again, she told me to stay put. She skirted away, and in a few short minutes, she returned with small box in her hand. She lifted off the lid. Inside was a lovely silver-plated picture frame that was engraved with seashells and starfish. The stock photo beneath the glass sent a wave of sadness through me. It looked just like the beach where Blake and I had made passionate love.

"They're very popular and on sale. Half price. Twenty-five dollars, marked down from fifty."

"It's perfect," I murmured.

"Wonderful." The saleswoman beamed triumphantly.

"I need to have it gift wrapped and sent."

"No problem. Follow me and we'll get it all taken care of."

I followed the slender woman to a nearby cash register. I paid for the frame with my credit card and then filled out a form with the address of Gloria's Secret's corporate headquarters in Culver City. I couldn't remember her home address, and there was no way I was going to ask Blake for it.

"Would you like to include a gift card?" asked the saleswoman, handing me back my credit card.

"Yes, definitely."

The woman handed me a small card, with the signature "B" for Bloomingdale's on the outside, and a pen. I flipped it open and neatly wrote:

Dear Gloria~

Thank you for sharing your magnificent beach house. And for all the beautiful lingerie and clothes. I had a beautiful weekend.

With my deepest appreciation~Jennifer McCoy

As I signed my name, my eyes grew watery. A tear dripped onto the black ink, smearing it. Some beautiful weekend. It ended up the ugliest, suckiest weekend of my life. Wiping away my tears, I asked for another gift card and rewrote my words quickly before another round erupted. I handed the card to the woman.

She quirked a smile. Again, I was grateful she wasn't too nosy.

"She'll have it before the end of the week."

I shot back a faint smile. "That's great. Thank you."

While she marched off with the frame and the card to help another customer, I put my credit card back into my wallet and adjusted my new backpack, which came in very handy being on crutches. Just as I was about to head out of the store, a familiar voice sung in my ears.

"Jennifer?"

Clutching my crutches, I pivoted around. My heart plunged to my stomach and every muscle scrunched. It was Bradley.

"Hi," I stuttered. *Get me out of here.*

"What happened to your foot?" he asked, eyeing me from head to toe.

"Nothing. What are you doing here?" My voice quivered.

Before Bradley could answer, a familiar saccharine voice sounded in my ear. "Sweetie pie, look what I found. Don't you just love the pattern?"

In a pained breath, she was in my face. Candace, Bradley's hygienist, wearing tight-ass jeans, mile-high stilettos, and a tight V-neck sweater that all but exposed her melon-sized boobs. In her hand was a large dinner plate with tiny pink hearts dotting the rim.

"Oh hi, Jennifer," she snipped in her singsong voice before placing the plate on the glass counter.

"Hi." I wanted to rip out her larynx and step on it.

She flung her left hand through her mane of brassy blond hair and then I saw it. My mouth dropped open.

My engagement ring! On her fourth finger.

Bradley flushed and then flashed his mega-sized pearly white teeth. "Jen—" Unable to complete his thought, he anxiously turned to Candace. "This place is a rip-off. Let's go to K-Mart and—"

Candace brusquely cut him off. "Oh, did Braddie Waddie tell you we're engaged?" Her possessive, predatory eyes sent daggers my way. "We're getting married in May. We just started picking out our registry."

I registered her words. An unexpected, sickening feeling filled me. My pulse quickened and then I succumbed to numbness. "Congratulations to the both of you," I spluttered as they argued over the plate. I hobbled away as fast as my crutches would let me.

This was all too much for me. I was shaking all over. I had to get out of here.

When I returned to my office, my already jumbled emotions were in a tailspin. My run-ins at lunch had totally frayed me. Yes, marrying Bradley *would have* been the biggest mistake of my life. But I was having second thoughts. Maybe I'd *already* made the biggest mistake—breaking up with Blake. Had I overreacted to the video? Knowing now about Bradley and Candace's insta-engagement, maybe I should have been grateful. Thanked him for sparing me an inevitable fate. On my drive back to the office with Libby, I didn't share what had happened or what was going through my chaotic mind. I needed time to think things out. Sort them through. Come to my own conclusions.

Back in my office, I did nothing but stare at the painting on the wall. *The Kiss*. All the emotions it elicited swelled up inside me, and tears yet again welled up in my eyes. There was a reason I couldn't bear to take it down. *Jen, face the truth*. It was loud and clear. As much as he'd deceived me, I was still madly in love with Blake Burns.

Was it too late to make amends? I'd shunned him,

pushed him away. Could I ask for forgiveness? Uncertainty tore through me. A sudden ping on my computer catapulted me out of my state of despair. Just before a rush of tears. It was an e-mail from Blake marked "Urgent" in the subject line. My heart hammered. I hesitated before opening it—half-hoping it would say something like:

Come to my office immediately. I want to fuck you over my desk.

Love~ Blake

Opening it, I shoved my glasses on top of my head. I read it quickly. My heart sunk.

Gloria Zander needs to move our meeting to this coming Friday as she will be out of town on the originally scheduled date. She will be here at 4 p.m. and is eager to hear about your erotic romance daytime block. Please have your PowerPoint presentation ready.

I shuddered. Blake's coldness sent a shiver up my spine. Not even a "hi" or "thank you." I had only forty-eight hours to finish the presentation. And Blake was over me. The waterworks sprang.

The next forty-eight hours were pure hell. An unbearable sadness ate away at me. Blake Burns completely ignored me, except for stopping by a few times to find out how my PowerPoint was progressing. His presence tugged at my heartstrings, and I fought back tears each time I told him it was going well, my eyes never leaving my computer screen. I couldn't look at him because I knew I would fall apart.

The truth: the presentation was progressing slowly. While I'd gotten most of it done before the holiday break, I still had some slides to prepare and needed to spruce it up. I had an impossible time concentrating. Blake Burns consumed my mind every waking minute—literally since I had to pull an all-nighter, something I hadn't done since college. I missed him terribly, but it was over. I unsuccessfully tried to convince myself it was for the best.

I finalized the PowerPoint at midnight on Thursday. My accomplishment lifted me out of my doom and gloom for a fleeting moment. I was pleased with it. Based on my instincts and Libby's focus group research, I had a convincing story to tell. Women 18-49 were craving erotic romance, and in the landscape of television, this programming was sorely missing. SIN-TV had a chance to create a breakout block of programming that would attract a new demographic and advertisers alike. Gloria's Secret was a perfect fit.

Bleary eyed, I got into my SpongeBob PJs and

crawled into bed, taking with me the latest *Hollywood Reporter* which I hadn't had a chance to read. It was important to stay current on what was going on in the entertainment industry. I quickly perused the trade magazine. When I got to the last page, which was a gossip page filled with photos of Hollywood movers and shakers, my body did its own moving and shaking. Staring me in the face was a photo of Blake with one of his blond bimbos all over him. Kitty-Kat no less. It was taken last night at a fundraiser gala at The Beverly Hills Hotel. While I was slaving away on my PowerPoint, Blake was out partying. Blake was not only over me, he had moved on. He was back to being a player. Tears bombarded me.

I tore up the magazine and sobbed my way to sleep.

Chapter 17

Blake

I was a basket case. A fucking basket case. It sucked to be me.

Why couldn't love be an open door? Jennifer McCoy was shutting me out of her life. Emotionally and physically. She was avoiding me like the plague. The few times we ran into each other, she gave me the cold shoulder and moved away as quickly as she could. And she kept her office door closed. I had to knock to see her. Glued to her computer screen, she never made eye contact with me. She looked on the verge of tears. The amount of pain I'd caused her was immeasurable. The amount of hatred she felt toward me unfathomable. I desperately wanted to tell her again how sorry I was and ask for forgiveness. And tell her how much I loved her. And then hold her in my arms and smother her with kisses. But her behavior made me feel like I was a persona non-gratis. It was plain and simple. She was done with me.

On Monday and Tuesday, I left work early. My beautiful tiger had eaten me up. Gnawed at my heart and torn it apart. Unable to focus, I drove home, drowned my sorrows with a couple of beers, and then crawled under the covers. Usually a sound sleeper, I tossed and turned. Trying to fall asleep, I even masturbated thinking about her. But wanking off didn't help. It made matters worse. Jaime's words spun in my head: *Don't give up on her.* But how was I supposed to do that when she'd given up on me?

Wednesday at work was no better. In fact, it was worse. More disheartening. I was going to ask Jennifer out for lunch under the pretense of discussing business, but when I popped into her office, she was gone. When she returned, she seemed even glummer and more unapproachable. She coldly told me she was working on her Gloria's Secret presentation and that it would be ready in time for our meeting on Friday. Before I could say another word, she asked me to leave so she could keep working. As I slogged toward the door to her office, I glanced at *The Kiss*. Surprised the painting was still hanging on the wall, I surmised it was just a matter of time before it vanished. Until every memory of me was gone. The sight of it frazzled me. Why the fuck didn't I just ravish her? Take her in my arms and give her a kiss that would make her fall apart? And fall again for me? She may have been a wounded tiger, but she was brave. As for me, the former king of the jungle, I was reduced to being a cowardly lion. My heart roared with pain.

I would have gone home early and crawled into bed again had I not had a fucking gala to attend. It was a fundraiser for an autistic children's charity my mother supported. Still vacationing in Aruba, my parents had called me and asked me to represent them at the ten thousand dollar table they'd purchased. As much as I wasn't in the mood to go, I couldn't say no. At six o'clock, I headed over to The Beverly Hills Hotel where the event was taking place. On my way out of the office, I passed by Jennifer's office. The door was closed.

I'd been to hundreds of these kinds of benefits. They were always the same. A cocktail hour followed by a long, boring ballroom awards dinner with bad food, drawn out speeches, and mediocre entertainment.

This was a very high profile event and paparazzi swarmed the cocktail lounge. I recognized many of the faces—close friends of my parents. Most of them billionaires, many of them celebrities. Drinking champagne, I politely made small talk with a few but stayed aloof. I wanted to leave.

A boyishly good-looking man about my age sauntered up to me. There was a slight swish to his walk. He was wearing one of those new fashionable men's shorts suits I wouldn't be caught dead in and was munching on some hors d'oeuvres. He looked vaguely familiar to me—in fact, I was positive I'd seen him at Jaime's art gallery party as well as the Conquest Broadcasting

Christmas Ball. I zeroed in on his tie. It was a Burberry plaid one—exactly like the one Jennifer had worn as a blindfold in that game of Truth or Dare.

"Hi," he said with a snap of his free hand. "You're Blake Burns, right?" I could tell from the pitch of his voice and manner of dress he was gay.

"Yeah. Who are you?"

"Chaz Clearfield. Libby's brother."

I twitched a smile. "Nice to meet you." I was in no mood for conversation, especially with the flamboyant brother of that annoying researcher.

"So, I hear you and my Jen—"

Before he could finish his sentence, we had company.

"Well, if it isn't Blake Burns."

It was Kitty-Kat, one of my former hook-ups, all decked out in a body-hugging cat-eye-green mini-dress. Holding a flute of champagne, she sandwiched herself between Chaz and me. She was right in my face.

"Aren't we rude?" snickered Chaz.

She sneered.

"Hi, Kat," I stammered. "How have you been?" The last time I'd seen her was at Jaime Zander's art gallery opening. She had stalked me.

"Great," she purred, pressing her big plastic tits against me. "I've missed you. Where have you been?"

"I've been busy." I wished she would leave.

"Blake Burns, can we take your photo?" another

voice called out. It was one of the many paparazzi floating amongst the crowd.

Before I could make a mad dash for it, Kitty-Kat yanked me to the side and wrapped her arms around my neck. "Smile," she said and then smacked her fat injected lips against mine.

FLASH! FLASH! FLASH! Shit. The photographer had gotten me kissing her before I was able to escape. As his camera blinded me, a chill ran down my spine. Who knew where these photos would appear?

I'd had enough of this event. Enough of Kat. I pulled away from her. She was miffed.

"Where the hell do you think you're going, Blake?" she hissed.

"Home." I said good-bye to Chaz who'd witnessed the whole miserable scene.

A short fifteen minutes later, I was in my condo. I took a hot shower and jerked myself off. There was only one girl I belonged with. The one I couldn't have. Jennifer McCoy.

Thursday was more for the same. There was no hope for Jennifer and me. Until I got a phone call at the end of the day from my grandma.

"Blakela, I ran into that girlfriend of yours yesterday. She told me she's *meshuganah* about you."

"She did?"

"*Vould* I ever kid you?"

No. My crazy, over-sexed eighty-five-year-old grandma was a straight shooter.

"Finally, you've given me something to live for," she moaned.

And vice versa. Telling Grandma I loved her, I hung up the phone. For the first time in almost a week, a glimmer of hope lit up my heart. And my cock twitched.

Chapter 18

Jennifer

The conference room mirrored the rest of SIN-TV. Sleek with lots of polished metal and black leather. Framed posters of current series hung on the wall along with the motto of SIN-TV created by Jaime Zander's ad agency, ZAP! "Television so hot, your screen will sizzle." And of course, a huge plasma screen was embedded into the front wall.

I hobbled into the room. Blake was already there, seated at the head of the large conference room table. His presence sent a shudder flying through me. Hibernating in my office over the past few days, I'd hardly seen him. Most of our communication was via e-mail. This morning, I had sent him my presentation to review and he'd approved it. The photo of him and Kitty kissing had set me back emotionally. I could hardly look him in the eyes. I hadn't expected it to cause me so much pain.

Despite the fact it was casual Friday, he was wearing one of his elegant, tapered, custom-tailored dark suits with a white dress shirt and a sharp looking tie. It had an unexpected, unnerving effect on me. He also looked rested and had shaved. His hair was back to having that groomed, just-fucked look. My stomach churned. Of course, he had fucked Kitty-Kat. And that was probably just for starters. Every nerve in my body sizzled.

His piercing blue eyes met mine, and I knew he knew he was affecting me. He flashed a smile. Why was he acting like nothing had happened between us? Why was he taunting me? I was an ice cube on fire.

"Sit next to me, please." His voice was authoritative yet seductive.

Pointing a forefinger, he indicated for me to take the seat just to the right of him. As much as I didn't want to sit anywhere near him, he was still my boss and I had no choice. Taking a much needed calming breath, I lowered myself to the chair and set my crutches next to me against the table. Blake rose, gathered my crutches, and then strutted across the room where he placed them in the far right corner. He returned to his seat, the heat of his body radiating and inciting me.

Seeking a distraction, I eyed my laptop sitting in the middle of the table. With the help of Mrs. Cho and our tech team, I'd set it up earlier in the afternoon to hook up with the big screen TV. Using a remote, I'd be able to project my PowerPoint onto the large screen. I turned to face Blake.

"Are you sure you want *me* to do the presentation?"

My unsteady voice underscored my insecurity. This was my first big presentation and I . . . we . . . had a lot riding on the line.

Blake didn't flinch. His hypnotic blue eyes met mine. *Get them off me!*

"Yes. This is your baby. Your pitch. No one can sell your idea better than you. Remember the three cherries . . . line them up."

The right idea. The right time. The right person. Blake's Vegas lesson—his father's credo. I had two out of the three cherries in place. The right idea and right time. I just needed to win Gloria over. A pang of sadness stabbed me. When it came to Blake and my own personal life, nothing was lined up. Everything was shattered. I fought hard to put what had happened between us to the back of my mind, afraid that tears might erupt. It wasn't easy.

On time, at exactly four o'clock, Gloria sauntered into the room with a stylishly dressed, spiky-haired man who appeared to be the same age. Thirty something.

Gloria was even more stunning in person than in the photos I'd seen both online and at her house. Tall and statuesque, she was wearing a black and white Chanel (so I thought) tweed suit with gobs of pearls swathed around her neck. Bright red lipstick stood out against her porcelain skin, and her mane of hair, pure platinum, cascaded in a loose thick braid over her shoulders. It reached past her waist. She was in a word—

intimidating. A magnificent powerhouse of a woman.

Her companion, blatantly gay, eased my angst. Dressed in tight leather pants, a vintage cardigan, a bow tie, and red high-tops, he smiled warmly at me. He reminded me a lot of Libby's brother, Chaz.

Gloria's eyes, one remarkably blue, the other brown, darted to the corner of the room where my crutches were stacked. Her eyes shifted back to me. I had no idea if she knew what had transpired at her beach house. I wondered—had Blake told his best friend Jaime?

Before I could push myself away from the polished steel table to stand up, she came by to shake my hand and introduced her companion, Kevin Riley, her partner and head of marketing and public relations. Her voice was commanding but warm. I instantly liked her.

"Where's Jaime?" asked Blake as she and Kevin took seats at the table across from me. I caught sight of her magnificent wedding ring with its entwined heart-shaped diamonds while she responded.

"He's still in Japan. A crisis with a client."

Blake rolled his eyes at her. "Oh, so he put his other client's needs before yours?" Blake had told me before the meeting that her husband's advertising agency ZAP! handled Gloria's Secret's media buys.

"Yes." A sexy smile snaked across her face. "He'll pay."

"Oh will he," chimed in Kevin.

Gloria shot Kevin a wry look and then turned her attention to me. "Thank you for the lovely picture frame, Jennifer. I've already put a family photo in it and set it on the piano."

I was surprised but relieved she got it so quickly. "You're welcome," I stammered, trying hard to quell both the scrumptious and turbulent memories of the weekend at her house.

"Why don't we get straight into the pitch," said Blake, his words rushed. There was no doubt in my mind—he needed to move on as much as I did. My chest tightened. Blake turned my way and handed me the remote. "Jennifer . . . " His voice trailed off.

Taking a deep breath, I clicked the remote and initiated the PowerPoint. Slide after slide spoke to the power of the erotic romance books I wanted to turn into *telenovelas* and to the research that supported my block of SIN-TV daytime programming.

I managed to steal a few glances at Gloria during my presentation. She sat at the conference room table poker-faced, her hands, with their perfectly manicured crimson nails, folded stoically in front of her, her intense eyes glued to the big screen TV. I also glanced occasionally at Blake. He was intermittently nodding with approval and monitoring Gloria's reaction to the presentation. Battling my nerves, I pushed myself forward until I came to the end of the presentation—a video clip featuring some testimonials from the focus groups. "A picture is worth a thousand words," my father, the wordsmith, ironically preached. I wrapped things up.

"So based on the popularity of these books and our research findings, I believe there is a huge market for erotic programming targeted at women. I'm tentatively calling the block, "My SIN-TV." *Done*. With an inner sigh of relief, I turned my computer off and anxiously awaited a response from Gloria or Kevin.

Silence. Gloria pursed her full, red-lacquered lips and then turned to her companion. "Kev, what do you think?"

I held my breath.

"I think Jennifer's idea is fan-fucking-tastic."

Gloria nodded, a smile widening on her lips. "I do too. I love all these books and so do Gloria's Secret customers. I think this a perfect match. I'd like to sponsor the entire block in exchange for product placement."

In shock, I shot Blake a glance. His eyes sparkled and a dazzling smile exploded across his face.

Gloria continued. "Jennifer, have you thought of an online component?"

"Not yet," I stuttered, trying to maintain my composure. Holy shit! Gloria Zander, the head of Gloria's Secret, the world's largest retailer of women's lingerie, had just bought into my programming block. Thank goodness, I couldn't walk because I would have jumped up and done a happy dance.

Blake, to my surprise, said nothing until Gloria spoke to him directly.

"Blake, what I'd like to propose is that we do an online joint venture. We replay the episodes of the *telenovelas* on our website and offer women a point and click opportunity to buy all the Gloria's Secret products featured. We'll split the profits. It'll be a win-win for both of us."

Kevin fanned himself. "Oh, Glorious, that's frickin' brilliant."

Blake nodded. "I agree. That's a great idea."

Wasting no time, Gloria rose from her chair and collected her monstrous Chanel handbag. Kevin followed suit.

"Blake, please have your business people call mine. I want to put this on the fast track."

"Will do," he said brightly as Gloria and Kevin came around the table to shake our hands. The deal was sealed.

Gloria's duo-colored eyes met mine. Rather than intimidating me as they did when she first arrived, they twinkled with warmth. She smiled.

"Oh, I almost forgot." She sunk her hand into her purse in search of something. She pulled it out.

My heart skipped a beat. Dangling from Gloria's palm was Blake's beautiful necklace with the pink tourmaline heart that I thought I'd lost.

"I found this at the beach house. It's not mine so I thought it might be yours, Jennifer."

"N-no, it's not mine," I spluttered, tears clustering in the back of my eyes.

"It belongs to me," Blake said coldly. He snatched the necklace from Gloria and placed it into the breast pocket of his jacket.

Gloria zipped up her bag. "Jennifer, you and Blake make a great team. Make it work. He needs you."

With a wink, she and Kevin disappeared.

While I'd won Gloria over big time, my victory was fleeting. My high had given way to anxiety. Being alone with Blake knotted up my stomach and had my heart flailing. Filled with the desperate need to get away from him, I pushed myself away from the table.

"Don't leave." His voice was a stern command.

I froze.

"We need to talk."

"About the presentation?"

"No. About us."

Every muscle in my body tightened. "There's nothing to talk about."

"Don't shut me out, Jen."

I held back tears. The door to my heart was locked. And it was going to stay that way for a long time. I'd had enough heartbreak in a month to last me a lifetime.

"Would you please hand me my crutches?" My voice was shaky.

"You're not going anywhere until we talk."

"Please," I begged.

"If you don't open up, I'm going to fuck you right here on this table."

"Excuse me?"

"You heard me right."

I trembled at the thought. "My crutches, please." My voice grew more desperate. I had to get away from him.

"Talk to me, Jennifer."

"It's Ms. McCoy. And if you're not going to get them for me, I'll just get them myself."

"Wait—"

There was no waiting. I pushed myself away from the table again and stood up. Hopping on one foot, I headed toward the corner where my crutches were stacked. Blake trailed behind me.

"Damn it, Jen. Let me in."

Oh, so now he was quoting lines from the movie *Frozen*. "Get away from me," I pleaded and hopped faster. Tears were now falling from my eyes. I was worn out and blinded. Halfway across the room, I lost my balance and stumbled. Fuck. I was going to fall flat on my face. In the nick of time, Blake clenched my waist, preventing me from taking an embarrassing and potentially painful spill.

"Hold on to me and I'll help you get your crutches." The tone of his voice was soft and repentant.

Reluctantly, I wrapped an arm around his broad shoulder for support and hopped over to my crutches, his hard body grazing mine. A chill followed by unwanted heat wound through me.

As I fixed my crutches under my arms, he cornered me, bracing his palms against the walls. He leaned in close to me, holding me prisoner. I could hear his heart drumming with mine and feel the heat of him.

"Jen, I'm sorry for what I did. I feel like an asshole."

I huffed tearfully. "You *are* an asshole. A fucking asshole."

He bowed his head. "I know."

"Now, please let me go." My tone was more weary than harsh.

"No, Jennifer. Not until you tell me what kind of game you're playing."

"What do you mean?"

"My grandma told me she ran into you the other day, and you told her you're *meshuganah* about me."

"I don't even know what that means."

"It means you're crazy about me. The way I'm crazy about you."

I narrowed my watering eyes. "I *was* crazy about you. And you know what? I was even going to forgive you for sending me that *vomiticious* video until I saw that photo."

"What are you talking about?"

"That photo of you all over Kitty-Kat in *The Holly-wood Reporter.*"

"Fuck." He bit down hard on his bottom lip and slapped his forehead. "It—"

I cut him off, my voice venomous. "We're broken up for not even a week and you're back to your old ways. I guess once the player, always the player."

"I swear to God, Jen, it wasn't like that. You have to believe me."

Tears stung my eyes. "I don't know what to believe anymore, Blake, except you excel at deception and breaking hearts."

"Jesus, Jen. You're killing me. You're the only one. I love you body and soul." He moved in to kiss me. Our lips touched briefly before I turned my cheek away.

"This is harassment. Let. Me. Go." My voice was tearful.

Cursing under his breath, he broke away and set me free.

With little satisfaction, I hobbled out of the room.

Chapter 19

Blake

Back in my office, I was numb. Jennifer had absolutely wowed impossibly hard-to-please Gloria with her pitch. She'd done exactly what my father preached. Lined up the three cherries—the right idea, the right time, the right person. She'd done a great job and I hadn't commended her. Nor had I told her that throughout most of her presentation, I was fantasizing about gathering her in my arms and spreading her across the conference room table and fucking her clever brains out until she admitted she forgave me and begged for more. Makeup sex.

I stared at the little snow globe she'd given me for Christmas. It sat on my desk right next to that *Hollywood Reporter*. I tossed the damn magazine into my trash can and picked up the globe. I gave it a shake and watched the shimmering flecks of snow dance around the golden ball. Jennifer McCoy had melted my heart, but now it was frozen. It stung like hell.

She had made it clear to me that forgiveness was not in my stars. Damn. Why couldn't she be more like her animated hero SpongeBob and accept me with my faults? Why couldn't she trust me? Believe me? Yes, I was seriously flawed, but it didn't stop me from wanting her and loving her. Setting the snow globe down, I anchored my elbows on my desk and sunk my throbbing head into my palms.

"Son, are you okay?"

My eyes darted to the door to my office. It was my father, back from his trip with my mother to Aruba. He was dressed in one of his impeccably tailored gray suits and sporting a rich tan.

"Hi, Dad," I mumbled as he strode my way.

"You're not ill again, are you?" he asked, taking in my feverish eyes and rumpled hair.

I shook my head and loosened the tie around my neck. "Dad, I need to talk to you about something."

"Let's go outside. Pour the brandy. I've brought you back a fine Cuban cigar."

One shot of brandy and a half-smoked cigar later, I'd unloaded my relationship with Jennifer on my father. He had the right to know as it could potentially affect Conquest Broadcasting business dealings. He listened intently with very few interruptions. He blew a curl of smoke into the unseasonably mild early evening air as I came to the end of my confession.

"So, I fucked up."

"It's not the first time. Is she going to quit?"

"No. She made it clear she wants to continue her

job. Her presentation to Gloria Zander was outstanding. Gloria's Secret is going to sponsor the erotic romance block she's developing, and Gloria even wants to partner with us on a potentially lucrative online venture."

My father smiled. "I knew she was a winner."

I slumped in my chair. "I'm the loser."

"Look at me, Blake." My gaze met his burly brows.

"I didn't raise you or your sister to be losers. Win her back. She's the best thing that's ever happened to you."

"But how? She's totally shut me out." I poured myself another brandy.

"Let me tell you a story about your mother and me."

My parents had the perfect marriage. It defied Hollywood expectations. After more than forty glorious years, they still loved each other madly.

"Well, it wasn't always perfect between the two of us."

My heart did a little jump. "What do you mean?"

"Well, in my day, I was considered a player too. Except they called it 'being a ladies' man.'"

I was all ears as my father recounted the time he had to chase my mother, then a young starlet but more of a drama queen, all the way to New York to prove he was in love with her. She had run back home after catching him with another woman. A rare moment of weakness. He practically bought her a flower shop and stood outside on the stoop of her parents' house in the pouring rain for two days, banging the door until she caved in. She let him in. The drowned flowers and all. My poor soaked to the bone father came down with pneumonia. Mom took care of him, nursed him back to health. And since then, they'd never been apart or stopped caring about one another.

I was in awe. I never knew that. The point of the story: You've got to go after what you want.

He took another puff of his cigar. "My old friend George Carlin once said, 'Men are stupid; women are crazy. And women are crazy because men are stupid.'"

Words of wisdom for sure.

"Women like slamming doors in our faces. They also like having them opened for them and knocked down."

Taking a sip of the brandy, I drank in his words.

"Skip Shabbat tonight and be smart. Buy her a dozen roses and go knock down her door."

And with that, I knew why I loved my old man so much. I did something I hadn't done in a very long time. I gave him a hug.

Chapter 20

Jennifer

TGIF. Thank God, it was Friday. Finally, the end of the day rolled along. It had been one of the most emotionally and physically challenging weeks of my life. A rollercoaster. A close second to the week following my almost-rape in college. Between getting around on crutches, pitching Gloria, and dealing with a broken heart that showed no signs of healing, I truthfully wasn't sure how I'd made it through. In fact, I felt more broken than I had on Monday. I should have been thrilled I'd won over Gloria and Gloria's Secret was going to sponsor my block of programming—and that was just for starters. But the truth: the victory was short-lived. The mere touch of Blake's lips on mine had set my heart on fire. My whole body was ablaze with an ugly wildfire that couldn't be put out. It kept destroying everything in its path. I was charred and marred. Tears burned my eyes as I wrote up a summary of our meeting—the last thing I had to do before heading home.

Libby was flying to Chicago straight from work to

do focus groups there, so I was going to have the house to myself. I had little to look forward to except getting my stitches out on Saturday. I'd be able to walk again on my own two feet and return to some form of normalcy. With the way my crippled heart weighed against my chest, I just didn't know what my new normalcy would be.

A little after six o'clock, I packed up my bags. I was missing one thing. My glasses. My eyes darted around the office. I frantically checked under my paperwork and then beneath my desk. I then opened and slammed shut a few drawers. They were nowhere to be found. And not being able to see too well without them didn't help a bit. Damn it. Where the hell had I left them? In the cafeteria? In the conference room? In the ladies' room? They could be anywhere. Giving up, I slipped on my backpack, which was roomy enough to hold my laptop, and hobbled out of my office on my crutches. Though I'd gotten used to them, I was so looking forward to saying good-bye to them tomorrow. Fellow workers I passed on my way out bid me good night and wished me a great weekend—yeah, right. As I neared the lobby, I heard footsteps running up to me from behind.

"Jen, wait."

Fuck. Blake. I hobbled faster. Giant steps. I'd gotten good with these sticks.

He caught up to me and stopped me in my tracks.

"You left these in the conference room," he said breathily as he lowered my glasses to the top of my head. His thumbs grazed my temples and made my skin prickle.

"Thank you." My voice was glacial.

He brushed a loose strand of hair that had fallen onto my forehead away. I clutched my crutches to steady myself. My body was a quivering mess.

"And you left this." He reached inside the breast pocket of his jacket. My heart raced, knowing what was coming.

"This is yours," he said softy, holding the heart-shaped tourmaline necklace in his palm.

It took all I had not to burst into tears. "I don't want your heart, Blake."

His eyes bore into mine. "But it belongs to you."

"No, Blake. Your heart doesn't belong to anyone."

He pinched his lips thin. "Just let me put it on you."

"Don't. Touch. Me."

Defeated and crestfallen, he slipped the necklace back into his pocket.

Tears were verging; I needed to get away from him. "Excuse me, please, but I've got to go."

"Can I, at least, give you a ride home?" His gaze held me captive.

"No need," I gritted, my heart aching. Without saying good night, I hopped away as fast as I could to the building entrance. Hopefully, Chaz would be waiting outside with his Jeep. Libby had arranged for her brother to take me home in her absence. I could always count on Libby.

There was no getting away from Blake; he ran after me.

"Jen—" He held me back. I jerked away and almost stumbled.

"Please . . . " He sounded desperate.

"Fuck you," I barked as I kicked open a door with my good foot and made my escape.

I thought it would feel good to say the two words I'd longed to say all day. It didn't. It hurt. Bad.

Chapter 21

Jennifer

Thank goodness, Chaz was waiting for me in front of the building. He helped me into the Jeep and laid my crutches on the back seat. Coming straight from his studio, he was dressed in a tight tee and studded jeans. The up-and-coming fashion designer always looked fashionable. After fastening my seat belt, I glanced out my window—half expecting Blake to still be at the entrance watching me. He wasn't. My heart sunk as we pulled away.

I hadn't seen Chaz since the Conquest Broadcasting Christmas Ball. Expecting him to ask me how my holiday had been, he instead turned to me and gawked. "Jenny-Poo, are you going emo?"

"What does that mean?"

"You look suicidal."

As we existed the parking lot, the dam holding back my tears burst. "Oh, Chaz, I'm a mess," I sobbed out.

"It's *that* man." He handed me a box of tissues from the dashboard, and I dabbed my face.

"You know about Blake?"

"I know about everything in this town. Libster told me what's going on."

I had made Libby swear she would tell no one at work about Blake and me, but I couldn't hold anything against her for sharing our relationship with her brother.

"Chaz, he broke my heart."

"Because of that video?"

Though that was only partly the truth, I nodded.

"Puh-lease. That was so frickin' brilliant."

"How could you say that?"

"He saved you from becoming Mrs. Douchebag."

"But the way he handled it was so deceitful."

"What did you expect him to do? Knock on your door and say, 'Oh by the way, honey, I saw your dweeb fiancé making it with his hygienist?'"

I blew my runny nose. He had a point.

"Jenny-Poo, get real. *That* man is the best thing that's ever happened to you. He's sex on two legs. He could make a dyke want a dick. If I could, I'd fuck him in a New York minute."

Despite my sorry state, I almost laughed.

"And he's crazy in love with you."

"How do you know?" I sniffed.

"Honey, I saw the way he kissed you at that Christmas party. No man kisses anyone like that unless he's madly in love. It was fierce. And I saw the way he looked at you at that art gallery opening."

The memories of those two events flooded my head.

Another torrent of tears touched down on my face.

"But, Chaz, he's not in love with me anymore. He's totally over me."

"How do you know that?"

"I saw a photo of him kissing one of his hook-ups at some big event the other night. He was all over her."

"Shut up. That's so not true. I happened to have been there. That bitch was all over him. I should have slapped her."

Every muscle in my body clenched. Oh, God. I'd made a terrible mistake. I should have trusted him. Believed him. But now it was too late.

"Chaz, I've totally fucked up. I've been so unforgiving and mean. I didn't believe him and told him to fuck off. He's so done with me."

"Honey, it doesn't happen that way. He's not."

"Oh, Chaz, what should I do?"

"Call him right now and tell him you know what happened. And tell him you love him."

I so loved Chaz. He had given me a glimmer of hope. I immediately pulled my phone out from my backpack and speed-dialed Blake's office number.

His phone went immediately to his voice message. Mrs. Cho's accented voice sounded in my ear. Instead of leaving a message, I simply hung up.

"He's not in the office," I glumly told Chaz.

"Girl, what are you waiting for? Call his cell."

Blake always had his iPhone with him. Sometimes

in the wrong places and at the wrong time. But I was past that. Without wasting a second, I hit that number.

His phone rang and rang and rang. *Please, please, please pick up, Blake.*

My heart sunk to my stomach. He was ignoring me. He didn't want to speak to me. I was right; it was all over. Finally, the call went to his voice mail. The sound of his virile velvety voice sent a shiver to the base of my spine. The phone shook in my hand as tears trailed down the screen. At the end of his message, I forced my voice to get past the painful lump in my throat.

"Please—"

My message cut off before I could even say his name. My phone had died. Shit. I'd lost battery power.

"Chaz, my phone just died." *Maybe it wasn't meant to be.*

"Use mine."

"No, it's okay. We're almost at the house. I'll charge it up and call him from there."

"You promise?"

"Yes. I'll call him."

"And then you're going to call me right away and tell me everything."

"I will." Trembling, I put my cell phone back into my backpack and pulled out my house keys.

Five minutes later, we pulled up to the Spanish cottage I shared with Libby. The lights were off. Chaz helped me out of the car and handed me my crutches.

He escorted me to the front door. The temperature had dropped. A thick cloud shrouded the full moon, making the darkened sky eerie. A shudder ran through me. It was just like the night of my sophomore year—the night I was almost raped. I forced the painful memory away as I inserted a key into the lock.

"Do you want to have sushi with me later?" Chaz asked as I unlocked the door, balancing on my crutches. "I have a Groupon for Roku."

Chaz knew how much I loved sushi, something I'd never eaten in Boise. But tonight, I was in no frame of mind to go out to a chic, celebrity-frequented restaurant where people went to see and be seen. And maybe, just maybe, I'd see Blake tonight.

"I'll take a rain check."

"Deal. When Libster comes back, we'll all go out—including lover boy."

"Sure." I quirked a little smile, covering up my doubts about Blake. I let Chaz hug me good night before entering the house.

The first thing I did when I hopped inside was turn on the lights. A roomful of shabby chic flea market finds came into sight and warmed me. It felt good to be home. Away from the office. I labored over to the couch where I unloaded my heavy backpack. I grabbed my cell phone and slipped it into a pocket. Crutches made carrying even the smallest things impossible. My stomach growled. I was hungry. I'd hardly eaten a thing all day.

I hobbled into the kitchen. It was unusually drafty. I turned on the light and noticed we'd accidentally left the window open. Closing it, I headed to the counter where I plugged my cell phone into the charger. It would take about five minutes for a signal to appear. My next stop: the refrigerator. Balancing on my crutches hands-free, I swung open the door. There wasn't a stitch of food, but at least, there was a half-empty bottle of Two Buck Chuck. It would have to do. Maybe some wine would help me relax and build up the courage to call Blake again. I reached into the fridge and wrapped my fingers around the smooth green glass. As I slid it off the shelf, a powerful hand clamped my neck. I gasped. The bottle slipped out of my hand and crashed onto the tiled floor. The sound of shattering glass exploded in my ear. But I couldn't look down. A horrific reality assaulted me. Someone was attacking me. An intruder. My heart pounded and I could barely breathe as his grip around my neck tightened painfully. Terror filled every crevice of my body.

I wanted to scream, but my vocal chords were paralyzed. What did it matter? No one would hear my scream anyway. Chaz was long gone. And our house was sandwiched between a deserted parking lot and an empty foreclosure. No one even walked their dogs our way.

Shaking all over, I felt my intruder tug at my ponytail, so hard I cried out in pain. He breathed in my ear.

"You're finally going to pay for what you did, you fucking cunt."

I instantly recognized the voice.

"Do you remember this?"

A snippet of dark, silky hair brushed across lips. My hair.

Oh God, no. It was him!

Chapter 22

Blake

I stopped at a flower shop on my way to Jennifer's house. Not far from my office, it was one of my mother's favorites. I had called in my order. A dozen of the most beautiful long stemmed pussy pink roses they had. And to my amazement, they even had the balloon in stock I coveted. A big SpongeBob balloon with "I LOVE YOU!" written on it.

While the jovial florist artfully arranged the roses in a large crystal vase, I wrote a note. I had thought about what to write in the car and just knew it was going to blow my tiger away.

My beautiful Tiger~

There once was a player named Blake,
Who found true love over Christmas break.
But when the stupid boy fucked up,
The girl he loved simply bucked
And left the poor bloke with a major case of
  heartache.

Be like your hero, SpongeBob, and accept me with all my faults. Love me with your heart the way I love you.

♥*nly yours~SpongeBlake NoPants*

Beneath my note, I drew a picture of a SpongeBob look-alike. SpongeBlake. Instead of wearing those dorky shorts, he sported a big cock. I scribbled a few more hearts around my drawing and then admired my creation. You know what? Maybe I wasn't a Picasso or a poet, but I had talent. I couldn't wait to take my tiger into my arms.

The florist slipped my note into a tall plastic card holder and inserted it into the vase. The SpongeBob balloon, held down by a weight, soared in the air, almost touching the ceiling.

Eagerly, I dipped my hand into my slacks pocket where I always kept my credit card and iPhone. My pulse quickened. The credit card was there all right, but my phone wasn't. Damn it. I must have left it at my office. I quickly paid for the flowers and then hurried out of the shop with the vase in my hand. I couldn't be without my cell phone over the weekend. Carefully placing the vase on the floor below the passenger seat, I put my Porsche in gear and headed back to my nearby office. Zooming down traffic-free Olympic Boulevard, I got there in no time.

Sure enough, the phone was on my desk. I hastily checked my messages. There were a dozen new e-mails and texts. All of them from my Vegas affiliate manager, Vera Nichols. And all of them marked URGENT, asking me to call her. Perplexed, I immediately speed-dialed her number. She picked up on the first ring. Her voice sounded panic-driven.

"Oh, thank God, you called me, Blake. I've been trying to reach you for the past half hour."

"What's up?"

"Don Springer escaped from jail this afternoon. I just found out."

My heart slammed against my chest. "Fuck."

"There's a massive manhunt out for him."

"Do they have any idea where he is?"

"No. He stole a car, and he may be armed and dangerous."

"Vera, I want you and your family to check into a hotel immediately. Don't worry about the cost. I'll take care of it."

"Thank you, Blake."

"Where's Eddie?"

"He's still in the hospital."

"Call the hospital and tell them what's going on. Order security. And take care of his ex if she's still there."

"Will do." She paused. "Blake, he could be anywhere. Be careful."

"I will." And then an alarm went off inside me.

"Call me if you hear anything." I ended the call and immediately called Jennifer. She needed to know. And I needed to know she was all right.

Her phone rang and rang. No answer. Fuck. She was ignoring me. Or maybe, just maybe, she'd misplaced her cell phone like I had. Or it was turned off. I couldn't blame her. She thought I was a prick. As I despondently slipped my cell phone into my slacks pocket, a horrifying thought crossed my mind. My heart hammered.

Jesus Christ. Had he gotten to her?

I raced out of my office to my car.

Chapter 23

Jennifer

His repulsive tongue licked my inner ear. I squirmed, but his powerful grip around my neck held me fast. Oh God! The man who had almost raped me in college was back. And I'd just made a startling, mind-shattering discovery. It was Don Springer! To my absolute shock, they were one and the same person. Blake had told me he was in jail, but he must have escaped.

He buried his head in my hair and inhaled. "Cherries and vanilla. Right?"

I nodded.

"Say it, bitch!"

"Yes. Cherries and vanilla." My voice was so small I could hardly hear myself.

"How could I forget?" He inhaled again. "So, it looks like you had a little accident."

"Y-yes."

"Soon you won't *ever* be walking. And you won't be needing crutches."

He squeezed his arm around my neck, so tightly I

couldn't breathe. My heart was beating a mile a minute and my mind was racing. *Think, Jen, think!* An impulsive idea flew into my head. It was worth a shot. I had no choice. He was suffocating me. Gasping for air, I silently prayed for my life. Then as hard as I could, I stabbed the tip of my right crutch onto his foot.

"OW! You fucking cunt!" Moaning with pain, he let go of my neck and bent down to rub his throbbing instep.

Yes! Clutching my crutches, I escaped, hobbling away from him as fast as I could. I had to get to the front door. To safety. And scream for help outside. Maybe even drive away. Then I remembered my car keys were hanging in the kitchen. I thought about dropping the crutches, but wasn't sure if hobbling on my bad foot with its boxing glove sized bandage would be any easier. Or faster.

Panting, I made it into the living room. Heavy footsteps were approaching from behind me.

"Get back here, you cunt!"

Oh God. He was after me. If only I could make it to the front door. I heard my phone ringing in the kitchen. It stopped and then rang again. Shit. Why hadn't I taken it with me? I could have called 911.

I was only steps away from freedom when he tackled me. I fell hard, flat on my face, crutches and all, trapped under his thickset body. Dazed, I tried to free myself, but his weight and strength made it impossible.

He had me pinned down. Fear like I've never known consumed me. All I could do now was whimper.

"Shut up, you little slut. I only want to hear you whimper when I fuck the shit out of you." He painfully pulled my ponytail again. "Understand?"

I nodded my head, biting down hard on my quivering lips to quell my sounds. Torrid tears poured from my eyes onto the hardwood floor.

He tugged again, this time so hard I winced. "I didn't hear you."

"Y-yes," I stuttered, my voice thin and watery.

"Good. You know, I could fuck you like this, but I want to see your pretty face when I rip you apart and come inside you." In one heart-stopping motion, he rolled off me and turned me onto my back. For the first time, I faced him.

Dressed in ill-fitting sweats, he was wearing leather gloves and a ski mask, just like he had my sophomore year. His insipid eyes shone through the holes, and I could see the evil smirk on his face beneath the fabric. I still couldn't believe my rapist and Don Springer were one and the same.

Holding my head down, he fisted my ponytail and dusted the ends across the openings for his nostrils. He inhaled deeply.

"I was positive I knew you somehow when I first saw you on the set of *Wheel.*" *Wheel of Pain*, his disgusting, sadistic game show.

He sniffed again. "That cherry vanilla smell of your hair always stayed with me. It took me a while, but I figured it out. It all came back to me."

As my phone rang again, the horrific memory of that college night flooded my brain. Of him shoving down my jeans, tearing off my panties, and unzipping his fly. And then snipping off my hair. I was shaking all over. It was going to happen all over again. If only I had my pepper spray.

"That wasn't very nice of you to spray that shit in my eyes. Or make me lose my job."

He slapped me hard across my face and I winced.

"And it wasn't very nice of you to stab my foot."

"I-I'm sorry," I stammered.

"It's a little late for an apology, sugar." He pulled out a large pocketknife and switched it open. I gasped. The razor-sharp blade was at least six-inches long.

"P-please don't hurt me," I whimpered.

He laughed wickedly. "This isn't going to hurt. I just want another little souvenir." In the skip of a heartbeat, he chopped off a three-inch snippet of my ponytail. He took a whiff of it and then put it in his pocket. The knife stayed in his hand.

I couldn't help it. I began to cry. He pressed the tip of the knife against my neck. Oh, no! He was going to kill me.

"So you want to cry?"

"Are you going to kill me?"

"Not yet. But I'm going to make you cry harder."

I was too frightened to say a thing. Just sobs. I bit down on my trembling lip.

"Now pull down your skirt."

I was too paralyzed with fear to move.

"DO IT!"

Shivering with cold sweat, I undid the button and slid the skirt over my hips. With his free hand, he shoved it off my legs. Then to my utter horror, he took the knife and slashed off the buttons of my blouse. He tore it open and sliced my bra apart. My breasts quivered as he ran the sharp blade across my nipples. Goose bumps spread across my trembling body.

"Please don't hurt me," I sobbed. "I'll do anything you want."

Through my tears, I could see him smirk again. And then he moved the knife to my crotch. Oh, God. I squeezed my eyes shut and just let the scorching tears fall. Expecting to feel unbearable pain, I instead heard another slash. I blinked my eyes open. He had cut off my panties and was holding them to his nose. After a deep inhale, he tossed them.

The phone rang again as he eyed my exposed center.

"Now I'm finally going to get myself some of that sweet pussy of yours." He jammed a stout finger deep inside me, and I screamed out.

"Shut up, cunt. And spread your legs," he growled

as he yanked out his finger.

I couldn't get my legs to move.

"Fucking do it, bitch!"

Slowly, I spread my shaking legs.

He laughed again. "This time your asshole boy-friend won't be around to save you. Chances are you won't be around to tell him all about it. And if things go as planned, neither will he."

Reality hit me with the force of an avalanche. He was going to rape me and then kill me. And then he was going kill Blake. Oh God. How could this be happening? The phone rang again and I began to think it was my always worried parents. Tears stormed down my face. I was never going to see them again. They'd never get over losing me. And poor Blake!

"Please, please, don't kill me," I sobbed.

"Jesus fucking Christ, SHUT UP! If I hear you say one more thing, this knife is going to be anchored in your heart after I shove it up your cunt."

I pressed my lips together and wept, trying impossi-bly to soften my sobs.

Gripping the knife, my assailant lifted his sweatshirt over his head, exposing his flaccid hairy chest and ugly paunch. But as he started to pull down his pants, someone knocked at the door.

"What the fuck?" growled Springer.

The knocking morphed into banging, and with a loud kick, the door came crashing down.

"You motherfucker!"

Oh my God. It was Blake! Holding a vase of roses with a SpongeBob balloon.

"Say good-bye to your girlfriend, Burns."

My eyes widened as Don lowered the knife to my heart, but just as it touched down on my skin, it went flying. Blake had managed to kick it out of his hand just in the nick of time.

"You're going to pay for that!" Springer leapt to his feet and charged at Blake. I was free.

"Jen, get away," yelled Blake as he defensively hurled the vase at Springer. It hit him in the chest and then landed in one piece on the floor. The water puddled around the scattered roses and a note while the balloon soared to the ceiling. It said "I LOVE YOU." Oh, my Blake!

"You motherfucker!" screamed Springer as he lunged at Blake.

Frantically, I crawled to the couch. A new kind of fear rushed into my bloodstream. As I watched Springer deliver one blow after another to my beloved, I feared for his life. A tsunami of tears assaulted me. My heart was in my throat. I could hardly breathe.

Struggling to ward off his assailant, Blake managed to reach for his cell phone. He tossed it to me, and it landed close to where I was stationed. I grabbed it.

"Jen, call 911!" he shouted.

I quickly did as he asked as Springer punched him

hard in the face. I cringed, feeling all of his pain.

"Fuck you, Springer," growled Blake, delivering a blow right back at him.

Their life and death battle escalated. Blake was panting and sweat poured down his face. The madman, for sure, had the upper hand. Oh God! I prayed for Blake's life and for the police to get here soon.

The loud blows went back and forth. Grunts and groans filled the room and mixed with my shrieks. Ducking one of Blake's blows, Springer grabbed the vase.

"Blake!" I screamed out. But it was too late. With a roar, Springer crashed it over Blake's head, shattering it to pieces. Dazed, Blake collapsed onto his knees, next to my crutches. Springer kicked him hard in the face, and Blake moaned. Blood trickled from his nose. I was sobbing. My poor baby! And then another kick. Blake, close to losing consciousness, swayed on his knees.

I couldn't take it anymore. Dropping the phone, I made a beeline for the knife on my hands and knees, crawling as fast as I could. God, help me. I couldn't let that monster destroy the man I loved with all my heart. My desperate pants sounded in my ear as I neared the grisly weapon. It was within my reach when suddenly it went sliding across the floor. Springer had gotten to it first and kicked it away from me. He directed another hard kick at me. Gripping my ribs, I recoiled and groaned.

"You little fuck," he snorted. "You're next."

"Blake!" I cried out as I watched Springer spring for the knife. He didn't respond. I cried out his name again even louder.

Clutching the knife, Springer stomped back to Blake. With his free hand, he yanked off his ski mask and hurled it across the room. The expression on his face was one of pure evil. I bit down so hard on my lip I could taste blood. My heart thudded.

My darling Blake had his head bowed; his eyes were rolling back. Oh God. I was about to lose him. "No!" I screamed out. Desperate, I crawled toward him, knowing in my heart I couldn't save him.

Springer, wearing that ugly smirk, snickered. "Say good-bye to your fucking life, cocksucker. You only have one thing to look forward to. After I fuck your bitch whore to oblivion, she'll be joining you."

My bleeding heart stopped beating as Springer crouched down, and the knife descended in slow motion. *Oh no, no, no, no!*

You fucking son of a bitch!" Blake! To my utter shock, he snatched a crutch and, in the mere blink of an eye, bashed Springer's balls. With a loud groan, the monster cupped his groin and dropped to his knees. The knife fell out of his hand.

"You fucker!" he shrieked.

"You won't be fucking *anyone* again," growled Blake as he whacked him once more in the balls.

Don cried out again, his ugly face contorting with pain.

Red with rage, Blake staggered to his feet, holding the crutch.

He spit at Springer. Venom poured from his eyes. "I'm not done with you, you fucking animal."

"This one's for messing with Eddie." *WHACK!*

"This one's for calling me a cocksucker." *WHACK!*

"And this one's for touching my girl." *WHACK!*

Springer was crying like a baby. Relentlessly, Blake whacked him again and again, moving from his balls to his chest and then to his head. Springer collapsed unconscious onto the floor. Blood poured from his nose.

"Fuck you, you piece of crap!" Blake grunted. After one more forceful blow, Blake flung the crutch and sprinted over to me. I was sobbing beyond control. As sirens roared in the near distance, he lifted me into his arms. Wrapping my arms and legs tightly around him like an inconsolable child, I sobbed into his chest. He smoothed my hair.

"Shh, baby, it's over. Are you okay?"

I nodded, the tears unstoppable.

"Talk to me, baby. It's me"

"Oh, Blake, I'm so, so sorry."

"Sorry about what?"

I met his gaze. Love so deep colored his eyes.

"About everything."

He kissed away my tears and then pressed his soft lips to my forehead. "Baby, there's nothing to be sorry about. We're alive and together."

"Oh, Blake, I love you so much."

"The same. Don't ever leave me, my tiger." As more sirens sounded outside, his mouth consumed mine in a kiss I'd never forget.

Chapter 24

Blake

I carried Jen to her bedroom and helped her get redressed. I'd undressed a lot of women, but dressing one was a first for me. She didn't say a word as she let me pick out fresh lingerie and a new outfit. I swear, I was going to burn whatever that sick animal had touched.

She was in no condition to stand up, with or without her bad foot, so I'd set her on the edge of her bed. I gently kissed her silky skin everywhere, hoping to soothe away the pain Springer had cause her. Sweet little moans spilled from her lips as I slipped a lacy bra on her and then helped her into a matching thong. Tears were still spilling from her eyes.

"Baby, you're still crying," I said softly, brushing them away with my thumbs. "Do want to talk about it?"

She shook her head, and her vulnerable eyes met mine. "I just love you so much. When Springer told me he was going to kill you, my life was over right then. Oh, Blake, if something terrible happened to you, I don't think I could live."

I squatted so we were face to face, just a breath apart. I traced her tear-stained face with my hand and gazed into her watering green orbs. "Baby, for you, I'm invincible. I'm *that* man who's going to take care of you. Protect you from the monsters of the world. Slay them if I have to. And no one's going to get in my way. Do you understand that?"

With a sniffle and a small smile, she nodded. She knew at this moment *I* was her superhero who would always be there for her. Not Superman, Batman, or Spiderman. No, me. Blake Burns. Yeah. *Thatman.* I took her in my arms and passionately kissed her. Yet again. Her hot tears wet my face as she melted into me.

After another soft exchange of "I love you," I finished dressing her. I trailed kisses up her smooth as satin legs as I inched up a full skirt and then along her taut torso as I helped her into a blouse. Her pink nipples peeked out from the lacy bra and I tenderly nibbled them.

She was still shaking. I'd learned when my baby was traumatized, she got chilled. After buttoning up her blouse, I put my jacket on her. It dwarfed her tiny frame, but I found it so fucking sexy. She was lost in me. There was one last thing I had to put on her.

"Don't move," I said quietly as I dipped my hand into the breast pocket of my jacket. Her eyes stayed fixed on me as I removed the tourmaline pendant necklace. Passion danced in her eyes as I hooked it around her slender neck. "My heart belongs to you, tiger."

She rubbed the heart-shaped pink gemstone between her fingers as if it were a magic charm. Then, she cradled my head in her soft hands and whispered, "Only to me."

The police arrived shortly. My brave little tiger told them everything. I was shocked to find out that she was almost raped in college and to learn her assailant and Springer were one and the same person. The sick motherfucker. A lot of girls had been assaulted by him and could now have closure. I had slain the monster.

Charges weren't going to be pressed as my actions had been in self-defense. There would, however, be an in-depth investigation. Right now, the police were more preoccupied with our well-being. One particularly compassionate female officer was concerned about not only Jennifer's physical stability but also her emotional state. She gave Jennifer a card with the name of a social worker who dealt with victims of sexual assault. With a faint but appreciative smile, my girl said she would definitely give this person a call. And I was going to be sure she did first thing in the morning.

The paramedics also showed up and wanted to take us to a hospital. While both of us were battered up, not to mention my big ass headache, we declined. They were especially concerned about Jen's foot and removed the dirty bandage. It seemed okay. She told them to leave it uncovered as her stitches were coming out tomorrow. The pain I'd caused her had already faded.

I had literally done what my father had told me to do. Knocked down her door. And thank fucking God, I had. If I hadn't gotten to her house when I did, that bastard would have killed her. I would have died too because *her* heart belonged to me. All that remained from my flowers was the SpongeBob balloon with the words I LOVE YOU. The vase was in smithereens, the roses crushed, and my clever little note blurred beyond recognition in a puddle of water. It didn't matter. Actions spoke louder than words. When I devoured her mouth and held her in my arms, I knew she was mine.

With the front door bashed in, there was no way Jen could stay at her house. Besides, it was the center of a major crime scene investigation. There was only one place she was staying. And with only one person. Forced to leave her crutches behind because they were part of the crime scene, she let me take her to my condo. She didn't need her crutches anyway. She had me. She belonged in my arms.

With candles lit, we took a bath together, another thing I'd never done with anyone but her. Her sculpted back against my chest, she sat in front of me, and we let the jets of my Jacuzzi tub soothe away our aches and pains and wash away the bad memory of Don Springer. I alternated between sponging her gently and smothering her with kisses. I also washed her hair with the cherry vanilla shampoo I'd bought because it reminded me of her. She moaned as my fingers massaged her scalp. The intoxicating scent made me heady. My cock grew hard beneath her. But I didn't want to fuck her. She'd been through too much and was still too frail. Her fragility tugged at my heartstrings. In the morning, she would hopefully feel stronger. I was eager to talk to her and learn more about what had happened in college. There was probably so much I didn't know about my tiger, but I was determined to discover everything about her.

After rinsing her hair, I stepped out of the deep basin and then lifted her out. I toweled dried her and then set her down on the double sink counter. I caressed her breasts and ran my fingers through her wet silky hair. She smelled so good. So cherry vanilla. Gripping the tourmaline heart in one hand, she stroked my face with the other and then kissed me.

"Blake," she breathed in my ear, "I want you." She wrapped a hand around my thick shaft and stroked it up and down. I moaned with unexpected ecstasy. I wanted her too. And my throbbing cock, Mr. Burns, wanted her beyond words. But not here.

Lifting her again into my arms, I carried her to my bedroom—my sanctuary where no girl had ever been—to the place where she belonged.

My big king-sized bed. I spread her across it. Even

with her bruises, she was a sight to behold. She looked like an angel. Love and desire glinted in her eyes. The fierce eyes of my tiger. I crawled onto the bed and kissed her everywhere. From her foot's wounded sole to her soulful face. No licks, laps, or nips. Just kisses, but the tongue-driven kind that let me taste every bit of her. She tasted fucking delicious. Trailing kisses down her torso, I buried my head in her slick pussy and kissed her delectable clit. Her body bucked just a little and she moaned.

"Oh, Blake. I need you inside me. Will you fuck me?"

Another kiss. "No."

"Oh." She sounded disappointed.

"I'm going to make love to you."

"Oh!" Her disappointment became instant elation.

For the first time in my life, I made passionate love in my bed to a woman I adored. We were side to side, face to face, eye to eye, bodies and souls melded. Her soft moans, our love song. A hymn. My arm draped across her sweet ass, I gently rocked her as my slow, sensuous strokes brought us closer to orgasm. The emotional intensity was as deep as the physical. Calling Dr. Phil. I swear, my eyes leaked tears as every fiber in my body screamed, surging to the edge of ecstasy. My cock was home. Oh, baby.

We came. She roared.

There was no taming my tiger.

Although I was sure I'd knocked off a few stripes.

Epilogue

Jennifer

My first upfront presentation. I had no idea what to expect, but I certainly didn't expect this. A full-blown event with hoopla galore at New York City's Lexington Avenue Armory attended by all of SIN-TV's key personnel, including affiliate managers from around the country, as well as by top advertisers. I was seated in the front row next to Libby on one side and my parents on the other. They had flown in for the event and to meet Blake's parents. Yes, my mother now knew I worked for a porn channel and my father had been right. While I actually hadn't heard her shriek when Dad broke the news, he'd told me that her "Oh Lordy" had scared away the mailman. Somehow, she'd gotten over it, and I had to say she was handling the upfront with its barrage of erotic programming clips and almost naked, well-endowed presenters quite well. Okay. She occasionally covered her eyes and look away. But I found this so cute.

Blake was a natural born showman. On stage, he was at ease, warm, and witty. And so damn sexy. He looked devastating in a brand new tapered charcoal suit with the jacquard tie I'd picked out for him. More than once, he stole a glance at me and my heart hammered. It was no secret at our office that we were a couple, but we were making it work.

After he presented the prime time and late night blocks, he introduced his grandma. I'd learned she was a regular fixture at this event and that affiliates and advertisers alike adored her. Wearing a gray velour jogging outfit and holding a shopping bag, she joined Blake on stage to cheers and applause.

"So, Blakela, should I tell everyone *vhat*'s new?"

"That would be a good idea, Grandma."

I held my breath as Grandma introduced SIN-TV'S new daytime block. MY SIN-TV. "Trust me, ladies, you're going to need *vun* of these. She tossed the contents of her bag into the audience. Fans! "Finally. Some sexy, *shmexy* programming for us *vomen.*" Loud gasps sounded in the audience, but you could have heard a pin drop when they watched the video presentation I'd put together with the help of Jaime Zander and his ad agency, ZAP! It included parts of my PowerPoint presentation to Gloria plus trailers for the upcoming slate of *telenovelas* and interviews with the authors and big stars who'd committed to them. Fifteen anxious minutes later, it faded to black. My heart pounded. Did they like it? Loud applause and cheers erupted. I even heard wolf whistles and shouts of bravo. And some were fanning. Oh my God! They did! My mom hugged me and Libby squeezed my hand.

Gloria Zander came up to the stage to tell everyone how much she believed in this block of programming and that she had committed major advertising dollars. Then, to my total surprise, Blake introduced me—the girl with the brains behind this "ballsy" block of programming. Standing up, I felt myself blush with an ecstatic mixture of embarrassment and pride. He asked me to join him on stage.

True to fashion, Calamity Jen almost tripped running up the steps to the stage. Catching my breath, I eloquently and humbly thanked the potential sponsors for their support.

"I love this girl!" exclaimed Blake. "And you'll be to be hearing a lot more from her. She's a fucking tiger!"

While scantily clad Gloria's Secret supermodels paraded on stage for the upfront finale, my man took me in his arms and smacked my lips with a passionate kiss. I had no idea how it was perceived. But I didn't care.

Blake

My father said Jennifer McCoy was the best thing to happen to Conquest Broadcasting in ages and the best thing to happen to me . . . ever. My old man was not always right, but he was never wrong.

Dressed in one of my tees and skimpy lace bikinis, she was snuggling next to me in the luxurious bed in our suite at the Walden Hotel where we were staying for the upfront. The five-star hotel was owned by Jaime Zander—one of his many holdings besides his advertising agency. Gloria and Jaime were also staying here along with many SIN-TV affiliate managers. So were my parents and Jen's. They were going out for dinner. And Grandma was tagging along. She'd promised not to talk about my *shmekel.*

A SpongeBob cartoon was playing on the TV, but neither of us was really watching it. Wearing just a pair of boxers, I was reading one of the erotic romances Jen had gotten me addicted to. *Seduced by the Park Avenue Billionaire* by Nelle L'Amour. Yeah, call me gay or tell me I needed a sex change, but I was totally hooked. Jen was deep into reading the script for our first erotic romance *telenovela* based on the bestselling *Pearl Trilogy* by Arianne Richmonde. The story: a forty-year-old documentary film producer falls in love with a much younger billionaire Frenchman.

"Are you excited about going to Paris?" I asked, tugging on her ponytail to gain her attention. Production for the movie began next week. Jen was going to stay in New York and then go directly to France to oversee the shoot. Cameron Diaz had been cast in the

THAT MAN 3   241

lead role, her first TV role ever, and some hot French hunk who'd I never heard of was playing the love interest.

"*Oui!*" She'd been boning up on her French and beamed a smile my way. "Are you going to miss me?"

"Nah," I said nonchalantly. *Fuck yes!* The thought of my tiger being away from me for even a minute drove me totally crazy. I'd become as possessive of her as I was protective—just like all those obsessed book boyfriends.

She set the script down on the duvet. "What if I fall in love with a handsome twenty-five-year-old Frenchman? Or the actor playing the part? He's single and was voted one of the sexiest men in the world by *People* magazine, you know."

Inwardly, I cringed. I'd never been the jealous type until I met Jen.

"You're going to pay for saying that, my little tiger." *Big time*. I was crazy in love with her, but right now, I was going to fuck her like I loathed her. No thinking. No mercy. In one swift move, I tore off the duvet and her scrap of lace and then yanked her smooth legs apart. With a savage growl, I mounted her.

"What are you doing?" she gasped.

"Punishing you. I'm going to fuck your brains out, Jennifer McCoy, until they hear you come in France. My name is going to be the new French national anthem."

"Oh." She smiled brightly.

The thought of wasting her made my cock instantly harden and swell. It was a lit up stick of dynamite. A fire raged from my groin to my blasting cap. Without wasting a second, I rammed it into her. She moaned with a mixture of pain and pleasure as my ruthless rod pumped in and out of her with ferocity and velocity. And I made sure she felt my teeth as I pressed my lips all over her neck and shoulders and marked her.

Her harsh pants and moans were like music to my ears. I had to let her know there was only one man in her life. Yes, one man. As they say, in French, *moi*. *Seulement moi*.

"*Assez! Assez*! I need to come," she begged in French, raking her nails through my flesh with one hand and fisting my hair with other. The pain only made me push my cock harder into her hot, drenched pussy, her muscles clenching each powerful thrust. Her nipples brushed against my pecs, hardening with the friction of my chest pressing against hers.

My mouth was a palm's width away from hers, and my eyes shone fierce on her. I tugged the heart pendant she never took off. "Tell me, tiger, who do you belong to?"

"You," she breathed out.

I wasn't going to let her get away with one-word answers. "Say: I belong to you."

"I belong to you," she rasped, her voice as desperate

as her need to come.

"Mine," I growled, the possessive beast I was. "Only mine."

"Yours," she panted back. "Only yours."

A satisfied smile slithered across my heated face and I moved a hand to her throbbing clit. I stroked it vigorously. Then, with a pinch of her fiery bud and another deep thrust, she shuddered all around me with a deafening roar of my name as I simultaneously detonated. My explosive climax met hers.

Oh, my tiger! I had captured her and was never going to let her go. After stilling ourselves, I carried her to the shower—where this time I fucked her the way I loved her with kisses and caresses. After the mind-blowing sex, we got dressed for the Conquest Broadcasting upfront party, taking place later tonight at the New York hot spot, Touch.

Before heading over to Touch, we had promised to meet up with Jaime and Gloria and several others in the Walden Bar for a few celebratory drinks. My tiger's daytime block of erotica programming targeted at women had fucking blown away advertisers and affiliates alike. Calling it "brilliant, breakthrough, and ballbuster," advertisers were clamoring to buy time in it. I was so fucking proud of her. Despite my initial doubts, she'd proven to me she was right and fought hard for what she believed in. Just before we left the suite, I told her that I'd left something behind. She shot me a puzzled look.

"Oh, it's just a little something for Gloria to thank her for all her support."

Jennifer's frown morphed into a smile. "Oh, Blake, you're so thoughtful!"

Inwardly, I smirked. Yup. That was me. Mr. Thoughtful formerly Mr. Asshole. How my little tiger had changed my life. I hurried back to the bedroom and yanked open the bottom drawer of the dresser, grabbing the bag with the little toy that was going to make her mine forever and off limits to any predator that came our way. Including any French frog.

My tiger belonged to only one man.

I was *that* man . . . that lucky man.

Jennifer

The champagne was flowing; our booth in the corner of the Walden Bar was a circle of raucous laughter and chatter. We were celebrating the success of the upfront. My block for a women's erotic lineup had been received with overwhelming enthusiasm. In addition to Gloria's Secret sponsoring the package of erotic romance *telenovelas*, other advertisers were eager to buy time on SIN-TV at a premium price. I had come up with a breakthrough idea that had opened the door to a whole new wave of advertisers. Blake and his father couldn't be happier. Or prouder of me. In fact, I had been promoted to Director of Daytime Programming.

There were ten of us at our table. In addition to Blake and me, our entourage included Gloria and Jaime Zander; Gloria's PR guy Kevin and his partner Ray, who happened to be Jaime's art director; Libby and her brother Chaz who was in New York for a fashion show; and lastly a powerful woman I'd grown to respect and love, Vera Nichols, our Vegas affiliate manager, and her delightful husband Steve. "Roar," a song close to my heart, was playing on the sound system.

"Let's play a game of Truth or Dare," insisted Chaz after popping another bottle of champagne.

The hair on the back of my neck bristled. Anything but Truth or Dare. The last time I'd played that game my life had changed forever. Blake caught me biting down on my lip and smiled. It had changed his life forever too. I wasn't up for this game. I didn't want my life to change. It was perfect just the way it was.

Before I could protest, Chaz's suggestion was met with loud claps and cheers.

A Cheshire grin spread across his face. We drew straws to determine who would go first. It was Jaime.

"Okay, what's your favorite piece of Gloria's lingerie?" asked Chaz.

"Darling, you can't answer that!" Gloria quipped, tugging at Jaime's tee. "It's too personal."

A cocky, dimpled smile flashed on her husband's handsome face. "Truth. Anything I can I bite off her gorgeous body."

Gloria gasped with embarrassment, then smashed her red-lacquered lips against Jaime's. The sight of them so in love sent a tickle of chills down my spine.

I was up next. I wanted to slide under the table. "Please, not me!"

Chaz shot me a fiendish grin. "Yes, you. Who wants to pose a question to Jennifer?"

"I do," said Blake, sitting cattycorner to me.

His eyes bore into mine. "Truth or Dare, Ms. McCoy? How many orgasms have you had tonight?"

I felt myself flush as pink as the Manhattan I'd ordered. I could hardly look him in the eye. There was no way I was telling in front of our friends, no matter how intimate they were.

"Dare." I shot the word at him.

A triumphant smile curled on his lips, lighting up those heart-stopping dimples. "Okay. I dare you to say yes."

I scrunched my brows. "Yes to what?"

"To this."

My eyes stayed locked on Blake as he dug his hand below the table. Oh my God! Was he going to stand up with his gigantic cock fisted in his hand and ask me to suck it in front of everyone? I shuddered. I wouldn't put it past him.

When his hand reappeared, I inwardly sighed with relief. A small glass sphere filled with water was perched on his palm. A snow globe. As I stared at it more closely, I noticed it contained a photo—the photo of the snow angel we had made together over Christmas. I stifled a gasp.

He handed me the snow globe. "Shake it, Jen." His eyes, glinting with a hint of mischief, stayed fixed on me as I did as he asked.

My heart did a somersault and my mouth dropped to the floor. I simply couldn't believe my eyes.

Sparkly flecks of snow danced in the water. But that was not all. Drifting among the shower of shimmering particles was a magnificent diamond ring. And not just any diamond ring. It was a large, multi-faceted snowflake diamond. Breathtaking! My hand trembled; in fact, all of me was trembling as the earth shook inside me.

As I fell further into a state of shock and stupor, the sounds and faces around me disappeared into thin air. It was just Blake and me.

While I sat there shell-shocked and speechless, Blake calmly took the globe from my shaking hand and turned it upside down. He twisted off the base, and using the index finger of his other hand like a hook, he scooped out the sparkling ring and set it on the table. My eyes, wide as marbles, never strayed as he put the snow globe back together and then set it down next to the ring. Around me, I vaguely heard my mates oohing and aahing. The ring was simply dazzling.

Blake's sexy voice brought me out of my stupor. "Well, Ms. McCoy. You haven't taken me up on my dare."

I couldn't get my brain to communicate with my mouth. Words stayed jammed in my throat. "Could you please refresh my memory?" I finally managed. I teetered between awestruck and dumbstruck.

"I dared you to say yes."

"Yes to what?" Dumbstruck was winning.

"To the ring." Blake paused and gazed deep into my eyes. His eyes didn't blink a wink nor did mine. In front of everyone, he got down on one knee. "Jennifer McCoy, will you marry me?"

The words whirled about in my mind like the tiny dancing snowflakes. When the latter settled to the base of the globe, reality settled in my mind. Oh my God. Blake had asked me to marry him. The tears that had been threatening began to fall freely. My heart was roaring so loud in my chest I could barely hear myself breathe out one simple word: "Yes."

Cheers and applause broke out, so loudly it was contagious and the whole bar joined in. Blake gently grasped my unsteady left hand and slipped on the ring. I couldn't stop staring at it.

"Oh Blake, it's so, so beautiful." I choked out the words. With my other hand, I caressed the side of his face.

"Like you, tiger." Happiness danced in Blake's sapphire eyes. He stood up and lifted me with him. Before I could say another word (as if I could), he yanked my head back by my ponytail, and his lips crashed down on mine.

In a fierce kiss. Just like the kiss that had started it all in a game of Truth or Dare.

And as I melted like a snowflake into Blake—*that* man who had dared me from the beginning to be his, I thought about how different my life might have turned out had I not accepted Chaz's outrageous dare that night six months ago. I knew at this moment life is full of truths and dares. Sometimes we have to eschew the truth to discover it. And sometimes we have to risk a dare. When life gives you dares, be daring. Be as brave as a tiger. Something rare and beautiful may reveal itself the way the moon does when a cloud uncovers it. Something that can change your life forever like . . .

Love. And melting as I was, our love was frozen solid. I had just dared to say yes to my new forever. And his kiss was just the beginning. *That* man was mine.

The End

NOTE FROM THE AUTHOR

Dearest Reader~

Thank you from the bottom of my heart for reading the *THAT MAN* trilogy. I hope you enjoyed it. And if you did, will consider writing a review—even a short one!—on Amazon or Barnes and Noble or wherever you found it. Reviews mean a lot to me and help others discover my books.

Would you be interested in a story about Jennifer's best friend Libby? Or hearing about Blake and Jennifer's wedding?

Let me know by e-mailing me at:
nellelamour@gmail.com

or posting a comment on my Facebook page:
https://www.facebook.com/NelleLamourAuthor

THAT MAN 4 and THAT MAN 5 may be coming your way soon! *Wink* In the meantime, I hope you read and enjoy my other books!

MWAH! ~ Nelle

P.S. Be sure to sign up for my newsletter to stay up to date on my sales, giveaways, and new releases!!!!
http://eepurl.com/N3AXb

PLAYLIST

I wrote much of the *THAT MAN* trilogy over Christmas 2013, so naturally Christmas songs, both classic and pop, influenced my writing. As some of you, dear readers, may know, I LOVE Christmas songs and could listen to them to all year round. I also saw the animated movie *Frozen* over Christmas with my twin daughters; the journeys of the two heroines and the hero, along with the songs, also inspired the story of Jennifer and Blake.

"That Man" / Caro Emerald

"Brave" / Sara Bareilles

"This Girl is on Fire" / Alicia Keys

"Ho Hey" / The Lumineers

"I'm So Sexy" / Right Said Fred

"Bad Romance" / Lady Gaga

"Blurred Lines" / Robin Thicke

"Roar" / Katy Perry

"Jealous Man" / Ace Moreland

"Bad Boys" / Inner Circle

"Have Yourself a Merry Little Christmas" / Frank Sinatra

"All I Want for Christmas is You" / Mariah Carey

"Drummer Boy" / Pentatonix

"Do You Want to Build a Snowman?" / Kristen Belle, Agatha Lee Monn, and Katie Lopez (from *Frozen*)

"Love is an Open Door" / Kristen Bell and Santino Fontana (from *Frozen)*

"Let it Go" / Idena Menzel (from *Frozen)*

"Crazy in Love" / Beyoncé

"Let Her Go" / Passenger

"Say Something" / A Great Big World

"Please Forgive Me" / Bryan Adams

"Love" / John Lennon

"The First Time Ever I Saw Your Face" / Roberta Flack/Céline Dion

ACKNOWLEDGEMENTS

I have so many people to thank. Trust me, it's taken a village to write the *THAT MAN* trilogy.

First, I want to thank my family for letting me write. They've had to put up with so much, including late-night dinners and pre-made ones that come straight from the freezer case. Thank goodness for Trader Joe's! My husband, despite his own busy schedule, has been especially helpful, picking up the mommy slack while I've sat, what feels like 24/7 behind a computer. One of these days, I'm going to watch TV again with everyone.

I am also grateful to my supportive beta readers who didn't hold back and gave me insightful suggestions. They include in alphabetical order: Michele Coddington, Tracy Graver, Cindy Meyer, Kim Pinard Newsome, Jasmine Roman, Nicole Scott, Jennifer Moshe Silverstein, and Karen Silverstein. I'd also like to acknowledge three dear, early readers who hold a special place in my heart—Amber Escalera, Kellie Fox, and Sheena Reid.

A big thank-you goes to Karen Lawson for proofing my books and making me laugh with her comments, Arijana Karcic for the beautiful covers, and my formatter, Paul Salvette, who patiently put up with all my revisions. A hug belongs to my writer BFFs, Adriane Leigh and Arianne Richmonde, who kept cheering me on. What would I do without your endless e-mails?

I've talked about the community of book bloggers in this trilogy. Writers, especially independent ones like me, are beholden to them. They work so hard to get our books into readers' hands. There are so many to thank, but I am especially grateful to Mary Tatar/Love Between the Sheets for organizing my blog tour. A shout-out also goes to those, who have gone out of their way with their kindness and support. In random order because I'm too tired to alphabetize: Cindy Meyer and Debra Presley/The Book Enthusiast, Jen Oreto/Winding Stairs Book Blog, Ellen Widom/The Book Bellas, Desirae Shie/Book Boyfriend Reviews, Lisa Pantaro Kane and Jennifer Skewes/Three Chicks and Their Books, Mags Pereira/SMI Book Club, Becky Barney/Fairest of All Book Reviews, Jennifer Noe/The Book Blog, and Sheeba Ellison/Bedtime Reads. Last but not least, the lovely Jennifer McCoy/Sub Club Books, who, by a strange fate, shares the same name as Blake's tiger. Talking about karma!

Finally, I want to thank my readers. You are so special and I love hearing from you. Your kind, inspirational words always brighten my day. You make every I-want-to-pull-out-my-hair moment worth it. I write because I adore you.

Thank you, all, from the bottom of my heart for being there for me. This is never an easy journey. I feel blessed.

♥ MWAH!

ABOUT THE AUTHOR

Nelle L'Amour is a *New York Times* and *USA Today* bestselling author who lives in Los Angeles with her Prince Charming-ish husband, twin teenage princesses, and a bevy of royal pain-in-the-butt pets. A former executive in the entertainment and toy industries with a prestigious Humanitus Award to her credit, she gave up playing with Barbies a long time ago but still enjoys playing with toys with her husband. While she writes in her PJs, she loves to get dressed up and pretend she's Hollywood royalty.

Nelle loves to hear from her readers.

Sign up for her newsletter: http://eepurl.com/N3AXb

Email her at: nellelamour@gmail.com

Like her on Facebook: facebook.com/NelleLamourAuthor

And connect to her on Twitter: twitter.com/nellelamour

Made in the USA
Lexington, KY
24 January 2015